CHRISTOPHER CARTWRIGHT

THE MAHOGANY SHIP

Copyright © 2015 by Christopher Cartwright

This book is protected under the copyright laws of the United States of America. Any reproduction or other unauthorized use of the material or artwork herein is prohibited. This book is a work of fiction. Names, characters, places, brands, media and incidents either are the product of the author's imagination or are used fictitiously. All rights reserved.

This one's for my children.

Elise and Matthew,

who are by far the greatest challenge and rewarding adventure of my life.

PROLOGUE

Southern Ocean, December 22, 1812

Muttering a vicious oath, Jack Robertson threw up. Again.

It was the most violent storm he'd endured since leaving England almost eight months earlier. The experience confirmed his vow that once he arrived at the settlement in Sydney Cove he'd never take to the sea again.

The Emily Rose shuddered dramatically as her entire bow lifted, losing contact with the white frothy water. It dropped off the edge of an enormous wave, before the following one swamped the entire back deck.

From below, Jack fell to the wooden floor *hard*. Then he vomited twice more before continuing to man the pumps.

Jack worked on his assigned pump throughout the night and into the following morning. His eyes drifted downwards. He, among so many others, had spewed until all contents of his stomach had been removed. This had then mixed with the sea water, which now mingled where his unsteady legs stood.

Jack could have guessed at the filthy state of the pump room by smell alone. Even so, he smiled. The watermark had been reduced by an entire foot from their efforts. It was disgusting, dirty work, but they were going to survive.

"Well, I'll be the son of a whore!" Jack said.

"Pardon me, sir?" Mr. John Langham asked.

"I said, God be praised," Jack replied, dutifully.

The ship turned abruptly, rocking onto its side, causing a number of people to fall.

What now?

Leaving the others to continue pumping, Jack ran up the ladder to the deck and immediately saw the cause of the sudden change.

A massive squall was coming directly from the south, and the helmsman was struggling with another on the wheel to maintain an easterly course.

High in the rigging above, a number of men were aloft, trying to quickly reduce sail area.

Boom!

Lightning struck the mast just before the fore topsail. The five men who had been attempting to furl it were killed instantly. Above them, another three men were trying to climb back down when the now damaged mast snapped under the force of the wind. All eight men fell into the water below.

The top half of the mast crashed into the water, but remained partially attached high up in the rigging. The sail area, having fallen into the water, was caught by the current. It was pulling the entire ship towards the rocky shore.

Jack could hear the screams of the men in the water below, desperate for someone to help them. On deck, he saw the other sailors' eyes were wide open, their faces contorted in horror, helpless to save the men.

"Mr. Mills," Captain Baxter's voice boomed.

"Yes, sir."

"Would you be so kind as to take some of your men and finish what God started on my mast before the damn thing drags us aground?"

"Aye, aye, sir!"

Jack watched as the young midshipman—maybe just fifteen years old, certainly no older—eyed the damaged mast, which looked as though it could snap at any moment in the squall. Mr. Mills organized a rope and pulley from the main mast to take the weight of the damaged foremast. Next to him, a man started to swing an axe as confidently as if he were on the ground in order to sever the remaining shards of wood.

Within seconds, the man had managed to cut through it and the massive broken mast swung from the rope, looking as though it was going to clear the deck. But at the last moment, the rope and pulley became entangled on the very tip of the yardarm.

"Christ, almighty!" the sailor with the axe cursed.

The rope needed cutting, but it was going to be a much harder, more dangerous job. The yardarm was basically a large tree log that sat perpendicular to the mast at various points to form a cross. From it, men in the rigging could unfurl and furl sails that sat directly underneath.

The problem was, now that all the areas above this yardarm had been destroyed, any person trying to get to the end of it would have nothing above to hold on to.

Through the downpour of rain, Jack could just make out the breaking waves upon the jagged shoreline. They were being dragged towards land. The sailor above must have seen it too, because he appeared to let go of all reservations and run along the yardarm.

The man pulled the axe up, ready to swing.

At that very moment, a large wave struck the starboard side of the ship and the man slipped into the violent sea below.

Jack looked to see who would now risk his life to save the ship.

No one moved.

Men were yelling orders everywhere and the Captain, whose voice was normally so calm it appeared malevolent, was screaming for the young midshipman to find a replacement to cut the rope.

And still, nothing was being done.

All right God, I'll go and save this ship – but then we're even.

Jack was an atheist, but fools who are willing to risk it all believe in hedging their bets.

He picked up the fallen axe, which had landed unceremoniously, lodging itself into the deck where its previous owner had fallen to his death. It took the strength of both his arms to pull it free. And then he started to climb the rigging thirty feet into the air where the others were trying to create a roping system to support someone when they climbed out onto the edge of the yardarm.

"Out of my way," Jack snarled.

No one questioned his authority.

Although no one on board could have guessed as to the extent of his violent past, most men aboard the Emily Rose kept their distance. There was something about him that suggested danger.

Jack crawled along the yardarm, his stomach churning. The damn ship seemed to sway even worse from thirty feet in the air. Crouching at the very end, he pulled the axe up and swung it at the rope.

The blade only cut one of the three main strands of the rope and then slipped past, the weight of it very nearly dragging Jack down with it.

He caught himself at the last second and braced himself.

Without waiting, he pulled the big axe once more and swung it down upon the rope. This time it connected perfectly, and the remnants of the massive mast and sail broke free. Below, he could hear the helmsman cry "Huzzah" as he regained control of the ship.

That was close. Christ, but I do hate sailing.

Jack shuffled back until he could hug the top of the surviving mast and then climb down to the deck below. He was greeted by the multiple pats on his back by the sailors who had failed to reach it.

"Well done, sir," the Captain said.

Then came the sound no sailor ever wants to hear.

Wood scraping along the jagged rocks below the keel.

John Langham heard the sound.

No sooner had its meaning registered in his mind than he saw the water spurting through more than a hundred holes below the bilge.

He stopped working the pump, a wasted effort. The ship was going down and quickly.

Instead of running up towards the deck, he turned and ran aft where the water was now already waist deep. It was cold, but he'd been working the pump long enough that it didn't matter much to him.

John knew he was risking a lot to reach it, but after all the pain he'd caused to reach this point in his life—somehow he knew, as though God had told him, that it was important to retrieve it and save it from a watery grave.

Worth risking his life.

He found his sleeping net swinging in the sinking ship. Sitting loosely on top he saw what he was after, his Bible.

He took a moment to inspect the vital contents within, then tucked it on the inside of his trouser pants. John looked at the companionway he'd come from. Water had now flooded that part of the ship, which creaked as if it were close to tearing itself apart.

His eyes scanned the other direction.

The water was so deep he would have to hold his breath to swim through some of the passageways, but it would be his only chance. He cursed himself for his stupidity and continued pushing through the now flowing water that was trying to drag him back down towards the ballast of the ship.

There was a loud crash, followed by the harsh vibration of the bow of the ship grating along sand and rock, which ended when the ship no longer had any forward momentum.

She's hit solid rock.

John pulled himself up through the final hatch using a rope to overcome the weight of the water, which flowed over him from his chest down.

He saw the captain's eyes—they told him everything he needed to know. They were done for. The Emily Rose was going to sink. His eyes cast into the distance—no more than three hundred feet away, he could see land clear as day.

Well, that's something, that is. But where on God's green earth are we?

Almost in response, the ship broke in two.

John fell into the water.

His hands thrashed about, trying to reach anything that

might keep him afloat long enough to survive. His head went under. As the next wave pulled him up, he managed another gulp of air before being dragged down once more.

It was dark, and the wave had spun him around several times before his hand reached hold of something solid. It was wooden. *Perhaps a barrel?* He gripped it with all his might and, despite being a poor swimmer, held on until he reached the shore.

There he quickly stumbled up on land. Sick and exhausted, John looked back at the wreck of the Emily Rose for the first time. Only the bow remained, sticking several feet out of the water.

Heads were bobbing near the wreck site. Some of them were accompanied by the frantic movements of arms attempting to stave off drowning, while others no longer moved at all.

Lord have mercy.

Lacking strength to help any one of them, he pulled out the Bible from inside his trouser pants and opened to the middle of the leather bound book.

Inside the cut pages, he was relieved to see that it was still there. A single gold ring, a small ruby embedded on top.

He held it up towards the light so that he could read the inscription.

ROSE MILLS 1810

He thought about the promise he'd made to the woman to whom that ring had belonged.

He would not dishonor his sacred oath.

※

Jack Robertson met the morning's sun with the confidence of a man who knew that he'd cheated death once more. Of the entire 138 people aboard the Emily Rose, he was shocked to discover that fewer than thirty had survived.

They spent the next few days collecting whatever supplies they might utilize to reach Sydney Cove. He found a strange happiness in their plight. A thousand-mile adventure through an uncharted territory. It was the easiest way to forget about what he'd done back in England.

The days were long and hard. They had to carry large amounts of food stores using packs. Water was scarce, the vegetation sparse, and the trees enormous. The country had a number of unique animals. Although plentiful, the animals had little meat to offer. What meat they found was tough and gristly. It wasn't an easy life, but they'd be able to sustain themselves.

After a week, the small party settled into the routine.

Occasionally, Jack caught a glimpse of a native watching them from afar. In general however, the aboriginals keep their distance.

It wasn't until their third week that Jack first laid eyes on her.

The Mahogany Ship looked like a mirage in the distance.

She was so large that her prominent bow and stern were visible hours before the survivors reached her. From that distance, she looked like a grand ship sailing through the mountain. At first, Jack mistook their distance from the ship. It wasn't until he was closer that he realized just how large the ship was.

"Christ almighty, I think we've just found Noah's Ark!" Jack exclaimed with awe.

CHAPTER 1

Gulf of Mexico, Present Day

The day was warm, even for summer. Sam Reilly looked at the sea below; it was calm, the rays of light glistening off the ripples beneath the helicopter blades. It was still too early for hurricane season, but all the same, he was keen to complete this case in time to be far away before they came.

In the water up ahead he could see what he was after.

It was painted sky blue. And along the ship's steel hull, in large emerald writing, were the words MARIA HELENA and below in smaller writing—Deep Sea Expeditions. From the distance, it looked like nothing more than an oversized tugboat or possibly an old icebreaker converted into a science vessel. On the aft deck a helipad could be seen—the only indication that it was anything more than a tugboat.

What couldn't be seen were the two most advanced submarines in the world. Both stored in its hold, Sea Witch and Rescuer One accessed the sea through a moon pool below the waterline of the Maria Helena. Nor could a casual observer know that it was loaded with some of the most advanced naval and observational equipment in the world, some of which would make the U.S., Russian, and Chinese navies jealous.

The sight of his ship made him smile.

Minutes later he was landing on the aft section of the ship, where several engineers eagerly awaited his arrival near the small helipad. Sam turned the main switches to off and waited for the whine of the rotary blades to settle, while his skipper, Matthew, approached. The man's shaved head ducked well below the spinning blades high above.

Matthew's hazel eyes and ordinarily serious face displayed a generous smile alongside his genuine pleasure. Holding out his hand, he said, "Welcome back, sir."

"Thank you. It's good to be back," Sam replied as he shook the skipper's hand and then climbed out of the cockpit, beaming with pride.

At six feet exactly, Sam Reilly had a physique more resembling a gymnast than a marine biologist. He was solidly built, with perfectly proportioned muscles, the result of a lifetime of strenuous activities. Of all of his adventures, the ocean had the strongest pull. He had brown hair in wavy ruffles, which softened his piercing blue eyes. Underneath which, he wore a smile, which most adequately portrayed a man who had it all, and was smart enough to know it.

He'd missed his ship and the people who served aboard. The man was by far the most conservative of his crew. Somehow, Sam had often thought, he seemed to take the responsibility of the safety of all persons aboard, as a skipper is obliged to, much too seriously. Their views had come to blows a couple times in the past year as a consequence. That aside, he respected the man very much, as the expert he was.

"So, this is our new helicopter?" Matthew mused.

"Sure is. I've just taken possession of her at Florida Keys. A Sikorsky MH-60, AKA, 'Knight Hawk.' Her long range fuel tanks will come in useful, since Tom destroyed the last one a few months ago. It's a little larger, and much more up to date. It also has a few additional toys, which Tom will like."

Entering the maintenance deck on the way towards the mission room, Sam handed the helicopter's maintenance book over to Veyron Blanc, his chief engineer. Having no relationship to the car whatsoever, the French engineer held a separate Doctorate in Mechatronics and in Submersibles. He was also one of the sharpest minds Sam had ever encountered, and in his line of work there were an abundance of extremely intelligent people. The man had little to do with the maintenance of the helicopter, but liked to be kept up to date with anything within his fleet of expensive machines.

Veyron took the logbooks, nodded at Sam, a gesture that he'd come to understand meant, *I'll talk to you later—I have a new toy to look at.* Like many engineers Sam had met, Veyron had more interest in mechanical contraptions than people. However, Sam was starting to discover that there was a lot more to his engineer than an almost autistic obsession with machinery. It was a side of him that few on board the Maria Helena realized.

Sam made a mental note to catch up with him shortly.

Genevieve Callaghan approached with thick European hot chocolate. "Here, boss. I thought you might like one of these after your flight."

"Thanks, Harry—you're wonderful. You don't know how much I've missed you," he said, embracing her tightly and kissing each of her cheeks.

"I missed you too, handsome." Her big brown eyes and long lashes, like those of a gazelle, greeted him with a look that appeared almost seductive with affection. Although, Sam knew that she, of all people on board, had no interest in him that way. "Of course, what you meant to say was that you missed my cooking!"

"That too."

Genevieve was a kind of Jack of All Trades on board, who managed the kitchen with an ability bordering on divinity. She'd once trained under a Three Michelin Star chef, but that was where, much to her parent's chagrin, her feminine attributes finished. Everyone on board called her Harry—after the violent cop, Harry Callaghan, AKA Dirty Harry—whom her personality and surname more accurately reflected. She was excellent at everything she did, an expert martial artist, athletic, and short-tempered as hell. For some reason that no one aboard had yet to determine, she also spoke perfect Russian.

Sam sat down with Matthew and opened his computer tablet.

Harry took the sign it was time to work. "Be sure to catch up soon, and tell me all about this beautiful girl I hear has stolen you."

"I will. You can bet on it."

Matthew smiled.

It wasn't like him to pry into Sam's personal business. "How was your sojourn in the Caribbean with that beautiful girl? What was her name, Aliena?"

"Aliana," Sam corrected him. "And it was great. But, now I'm here again, and that means it's time to get back to work and solve this disaster—before hurricane season really takes off and it becomes a problem for all of us."

"Understood."

Sam looked around the otherwise empty mission room and asked, "Where is he?"

"Who?"

"Tom Bower."

"He's still below on a dive—should be up soon."

"Good, get him back up here. I want him to bring me up to speed with our problem and what he's done about it." Sam looked at Matthew and said, "What have we got so far?"

Matthew gave a quick whistle, and a man monitoring the dive gave the signal for Tom to return to ship.

Matthew then turned on the overhead projector.

"As you know, summer can be a tough time for many species in the Gulf of Mexico, when the combination of nutrient-rich river runoff and warm temperatures can rob coastal bottom waters of oxygen. Where that happens, shrimp, fish, and other creatures can be forced to flee to fresher waters, leaving a so-called 'Dead Zone' behind."

"I read the report. I've heard about them, but didn't know a lot about those that affected the Gulf of Mexico. Here, the Dead Zones are caused by runoff from land rich in nutrients such as nitrogen and phosphorous. These elements aren't toxic, but they are potent fertilizers. In fact, in the Mississippi River, which drains about forty percent of the continental United States and most of its Midwestern farmland, agricultural fertilizers are the main source of these elements. Air pollution and urban development also increase nutrient runoff. When these nutrients find their way to the Gulf of Mexico they cause unnaturally large algal blooms. The algae then die and sink to the bottom, where they're decomposed by oxygen-consuming bacteria. During the warm summer months, when there is little mixing in the water column, the bottom water can stagnate and become hypoxic, or low in oxygen. If the hypoxia becomes severe enough, you have a Dead Zone." Sam wasn't reading from notes—he had a memory bordering on photographic. "So, what's so different about it this time?"

"Well, I'll show you. See here? This is a normal graph of a

typical summer Dead Zone. See the purple markings? They represent the Dead Zone for last year."

Sam followed the graph along the coastal region of up to two miles off shore from the numerous landfalls, which make up the Gulf of Mexico, "And this year?"

"Check this out . . ."

In front of him, the projector displayed an image of the entire Gulf of Mexico covered in red.

There must be a mistake. If this is right, the world is in for serious trouble!

"Are you sure that's right?"

"It's right—and to make matters worse, normally this only affects ground feeding fish, such as shrimp, crustaceans, etc. But this year we're talking about widespread devastation of sea life."

"And at the current rate, if we can't stop the progression?"

"The world's oceans will be rendered inhospitable to all but the most resilient of sea creatures within two to three years."

"Do we have any idea what's causing their demise?"

"Yes, and no." Matthew looked worried.

Sam knew why. He was a kind boss, but he wanted answers, and had little time for people sitting on the fence. "All right, what do we know?"

"Analysis of the dead sea creatures show that they have been affected with hydrogen cyanide."

"The Mexican silver mines?" Sam realized instantly.

"Probably, but it will be hard to prove."

"Why? Where's the primary source of the contamination?"

"Tom's managed to trace the source of their original

contamination to a location below us—about three hundred feet to be exact."

"Someone's been dumping something they shouldn't?"

"That's what we thought at first, but not necessarily. It looks like something way more interesting than that."

"What is it?"

"No, Tom would kill me if I took away all his thunder," Matthew complained.

"Forget Tom. I'm the one paying for this project."

"Who wants to forget me?" Tom said as he walked in, his dive suit still dripping wet.

"I do, you tall bastard."

Tom was stoked to see Sam again, and his big, cheeky grin beamed from ear to ear while he shook Sam's hand. It was solid. Not the type of handshake where a man tries to impress another with the strength of his grip, but instead, simply the firm handshake of a man whose hands were as strong as a vice.

It had only been a week, but the project just didn't feel right without Sam. And then, after his most recent dive, he couldn't believe his buddy missed it. Sam was going to be pissed when he discovered this was more than a simple case of someone dumping something they shouldn't in an environment that couldn't deal with it.

His wetsuit was still dripping, having come straight up from the ship's moon pool. When his boss said come now, he didn't wait to get dry.

"Good to see you, Sam," he said, giving his friend a giant bear hug.

"You too, Tom. Now, what have you got for me?"

He expected such a reply from Sam—the man was focused when he started a new project.

"You're not going to believe what we've found."

"Try me."

"Okay, so the cause of this year's apocalyptic Dead Zone was hydrogen cyanide . . ."

"Yeah, yeah . . ." Sam interrupted his thunder. "Often used in mining, probably one of the local Mexican silver mines."

"Okay, so I see Matthew's filled you in. But the next part is what you're going to find really interesting, my friend."

"What?"

"The sources of the contamination weren't dumped here at all, as we expected. Instead, it came from an underwater tunnel, and guess who owned the tunnel?"

"Michael Rodriguez, the owner of the closest silver mine?"

"Good guess, but no. A man by the name of Ajtzak Wikea."

He waited for the name to ring a bell in Sam's ear, but it didn't.

"Never heard of him. What does he do?"

"Not what he does, but what he did." Waiting for the words to sink in, Tom continued, "He lost the future hope of the Mayan empire, after losing its greatest weapon at the Ciudad Del Carmen in 1443 to an unknown enemy."

Sam's eyes focused and his smile turned radiant, "The Ark of Light—I've read about it, and often wondered if there was any truth to the stories. Myth has it that it was a powerful scepter, covered with ornate jewels, and at the center a giant diamond, which had the ability to regulate the direction and intensity of the sun. Enough power to destroy ships with one shot—but it's never been found, and neither has any evidence of its existence. Like all longstanding myths, I can imagine that its origins had some semblance of truth."

"That's the one . . ."

"What else do we know about Ciudad Del Carmen?"

"Not a lot. So far, all we know is little more than what the tourist brochure says—that what was named "Ciudad Del Carmen" in the 16th century by the Spanish invaders, was a Mayan fortress dating back thousands of years that served as a trading outpost between the Aztec and Mayan civilizations."

"Do we have the archeological maps of the Mayan fortress?"

"Sure do. It took some work, but we convinced someone from the University of Mexico to email them to us."

"And what did they show?" Sam asked.

"Nothing that would indicate an underground passage deep below the sea."

"So what we've found is an entirely new section of the building?"

"Looks like it."

"Okay, so how did our fifteenth century friend get involved in all this?" Sam asked, shaking his head.

"That I don't know. But the tunnel leads somewhere, and I think it's time you and I find out where—so we can stop this before it destroys most of the planet's sea life."

"Sounds like a plan. When do we dive?"

"The Rock will be ready in two hours."

A crooked smile crossed Sam's face, as he thought about

diving the unexplored, ancient Mayan tunnel.

This was more like the environment he wanted to work in: dangerous, mysterious, and ancient. He went through the dive plan with Tom, and although he now took over the control of the mission, he was happy with the plan.

They would use the dive bell to reach the seafloor, 300 feet below. The Maria Helena housed a technologically advanced dive bell. It was capable of supporting up to five divers at any one time for up to five days without shipside support, or indefinitely with a shipside tether.

The Rock, as the bell was affectionately known, had a potential bottom depth range of 1000 feet, although Sam would be reluctant to attempt to work at such depths without the aid of a mechanical atmospheric dive suit. It was also equipped with a hyperbaric chamber, making rapid ascents possible, if required.

Once on the seabed, Sam and Tom would set up for a deep dive and enter the tunnel. Wearing fully encapsulated diving helmets, the two men would be protected from the lethality of the hydrogen cyanide, which is most dangerous when breathed or ingested. At that depth, the two men would have a dive time of less than fifty minutes in which to locate the source of the cyanide contamination and seal it. Returning to the outer chamber of the Rock, the two men could then begin the decontamination process, which involved scrubbing each dive suit with a neutralizing agent before entering the dive bell and then having the dive suit washed again before the men removed the equipment and entered the main living area of the bell.

Or that was how it was supposed to go.

At the bottom of the seafloor Sam shook Tom, who, lying flat on his back in the relatively cramped space, was snoring soundly. It took more than a light shake to rouse the man,

"Hey, we're here. It's time to get ready."

"What time is it?" Tom's voice was groggy.

"1410. The dive time is set to commence at 1430." Shaking his head, Sam said, "We're about to dive in 300 feet of water. Our bodies will be under 30 times their normal atmospheric pressure. As though that isn't dangerous enough, we're going to do so in the hope of sealing a catastrophic leak of hydrogen cyanide, in a tunnel that will compete with the extreme depth to kill us . . . and yet you sleep like a baby?"

Tom shrugged his shoulders, "I've always been a good sleeper — you never know when you'll need the extra energy later. You want an egg sandwich before we dive? I packed you one too," he said casually, taking a bite.

"I'll be all right, but make it quick."

Sam put his legs through his dry suit and checked both of their twin dive tanks. By the time he looked up, he caught a glimpse of Tom shoving the remaining half of his sandwich in his mouth. His boyish grin was displayed behind the mouth full of food.

Ordinarily, Sam would remain on the ship as the director of the operation. But when Tom had spoken of an ancient tunnel, he wouldn't hear a word about missing out on it. Consequently, Matthew would take over his role. He had direct access with several doctors from the CDC, who could provide real time answers to any question Sam or Tom asked while they were in the tunnel.

It took less than five minutes to lock their dive helmets and complete their checks on each other before they were ready to dive.

"Maria Helena, Maria Helena, this is Reilly, how do you read?" Sam said through his push to talk (PTT) system.

"Loud and clear." It was Matthew's voice that answered

him.

"Very good. Now that we've established the Rock's relay communications are working, are we clear to dive?"

"Weather up here is still good. You and Tom have a safe dive."

Sam looked at Tom, who nodded to show he was ready. And then, one after the other, they started to climb backwards down the steps into the moon pool below, and into another world.

The water was dark, but the visibility with their flashlights excellent — at least fifty feet. Sam checked that the navigation beacon on board the Rock was working, and that his range finder could clearly see it. Reassured by the flashing bulb, he then held the electronic dive tablet in front of him, and hit Search.

It flashed several times, sending ultrahigh frequency sound waves out in a 270-degree arc ahead of them. Immediately, the screen showed the flat surface of the seabed and the only obstacle for a hundred feet — the entrance to the tunnel.

Sam pointed at his marking, and Tom responded, "That's our cave."

"Copy that." He marked the entrance to the tunnel with an asterisk, and like a GPS his tablet directed him precisely to the point.

"Just wait till you see this thing, Sam . . ." Tom said.

It was a short swim to the entrance of the tunnel. The surrounding area was noticeably devoid of any sea life.

Sam looked up at the entrance in front of him.

"Holy shit, you've got to be kidding me!"

Above him, the entrance to the tunnel stood at nearly forty feet. The outside was carved in ornate jade, intricately connected. Despite the buildup of sand and erosion of nearly six centuries, Sam had no doubt what he was looking at. His mind quickly referenced the little he knew about Mayan culture.

This was no tunnel.

It was something entirely different—the very top of a pyramid.

At the opening stood a golden sculpture. The size of a large man, it held a spear pointing out towards a distant enemy. No light reached this spot, but as Sam focused his flashlight towards it, the spear glowed. Only it wasn't a spear, at all.

"Do you realize what that is?" Sam said, already kicking his fins towards the ancient artefact.

"Like I said, The Ark of Light was real."

Sam was certain the second he saw it.

A man who was quick to assess a situation, but slow and confident with a decision, he was used to being correct. It was because of this that the disappointment was so strong when he reached the structure and discovered it was nothing more than a sculpture, with a piece of glass at its center. Still doubting himself, Sam wondered if it was made of diamond, instead.

"Sorry, Sam," Tom said, "I thought I told you I'd already searched the entrance? Even I would have noticed if it were the real Ark of Light."

"It's okay. I just got my hopes up."

"Do you think we'll find what old Ajtzak did with the Ark of Light somewhere inside this tunnel?" Tom asked.

"I've no idea, but I think this is the closest that mankind has come to discovering the weapon since it was lost in the fifteenth century." Sam examined the structure of the entrance with admiration. "And something tells me this was never meant as a tunnel..."

"What then?"

"A tomb—Maybe Ajtzak's final resting place? There was nothing in the history books about where they buried him, or even if he was given a King's burial, as his bloodline suggested he should."

"You might just be on to something there."

"I'm certain of it," Sam said. "What I can't work out though, is how a fifteenth century civilization managed to build anything at a depth of 300 feet of water, especially something this intricate."

"Maybe they built it on land and then lowered it off a massive ship?"

"No, even if they had the means of carrying something this large on a ship, there's no way they could have sunk it and had it land so perfectly."

"How then?"

"Let's go find out."

"Agreed."

They swam inside the entrance of the pyramid, which was much less elaborate than its outside. The tunnel could just have easily been a flooded subway in New York for all the similarities of appearance. They swam downwards nearly thirty feet and then found one long tunnel heading both west and east.

"Diver Reilly, radio check Maria Helena?"

"Hearing you a little weak, say again."

Sam stuck a relay transmitter and booster to the tunnel wall.

"How do you read me now, Matthew?"

"Loud and clear."

"Good. What we have here appears to be the top of an ancient pyramid, probably Mayan given its location. All we could see from the entrance was the very top, surrounded by sand. There's no way to guess how much further down this may go. The water here has the highest concentrations of hydrogen cyanide, so at least we're onto something with our first mission — to seal the leak and contain the contamination. We're going to explore this tunnel and see what we find."

"Very good, keep us in communication range."

"Will do."

Sam looked at Tom, and said, "Let's separate. You want to go east or west first?"

"East."

"Okay, make certain you stay within radio range."

"Will do, boss — you just call when you need me to rescue your ass."

"You can count on it."

The tunnel went for approximately 80 feet from one end to the other. At each end, the tunnel submerged further in a steep downward direction, as though the top of the outside pyramid was just the tip of the iceberg, which extended deep into the seabed.

Of course, that would be impossible . . .

"What do you want to do, Sam?"

"Plant another transmitter, and if you're happy, let's continue further down. I have a crazy feeling that we might just meet at the bottom. If you lose radio reception, double back, and meet at the Rock. I don't want to take any chances."

"Sounds like a plan."

Sam continued down the steep tunnel. There were boulders on either side, suggesting that whoever once built it, used stone to prop up the walls. *Or that someone had actually built a real pyramid here first and then it was filled with water?* Sam brushed the idea from his mind. It didn't even warrant contemplation.

Sam checked his dive watch.

He was already 480 feet underwater. Their decompress time was going to be pretty long, not that Sam worried about that. He had the Rock, after all. It was his remaining Hydrox that worried him.

"How's your Hydrox levels, Tom?"

"I've got another 40 minutes at this depth, how about you?"

"Same. Let's just make sure we've got plenty of time to make the return. I have no intention of joining any king in his burial tomb."

"I'm with you there."

At 240 feet, the angle of the tunnel turned abruptly inwards, and the tunnel was once again horizontal.

"Your tunnel horizontal again, Tom?"

"Yeah, you too?"

"Yeah, it may have been just a tunnel, but it's one hell of a deep tunnel, all the same. How any civilization worked out how to dig this beats me!"

"I've heard you use that voice before. You're going to have to find out aren't you? It will be Zanzibar all over again, won't it?"

Sam smiled to himself as he shook his head, recalling the events of their discovery in Zanzibar last year. *There's no way I could be so wrong – twice.*

"They'll find how it was done one day, let me assure you. I

just hope I live long enough to have my answer. Hey, I think I can see your light up ahead."

"That's not possible," Tom's voice was calm, but deadly serious.

"Why not?"

"Because I turned mine off more than a minute ago, when I saw your light."

CHAPTER 2

Tom was so distracted by the brightness of the light, that he nearly missed the crack in the outer wall entirely. When the current grabbed him, he thought it was a monster of the deep drawing him into its jaws.

He would have been amazed to learn that the crack was no larger than his hand, but the extreme pressure gradient expelled the fluid like a jet. If he'd had time to prepare, he would have been able to brace himself, or at least avoid the direct point of flow.

Spinning from the pressure, his buoyancy disorientated by the flow, Tom's helmet collided with the masonry of the tunnel wall, directly opposite to the crack.

Gas instantly began erupting from the fissure.

"Shit, my helmet's been compromised . . ." he yelled, but no one heard his words. His radio, along with his faceplate, were destroyed.

Hydrox, the oxygen rich hydrogen gas designed for deep sea diving, flowed freely from his faceplate. The bubbles it created blinded him completely. With the high concentrations of hydrogen cyanide in his surrounding water, it was the positive pressure of the Hydrox that was still keeping him alive, but it would expire within minutes at this rate.

Tom flicked his flashlight on and off continuously. He had no idea which direction in relation to himself Sam was, but he knew that a message had to be passed, if he was ever going to see the surface. If he'd thought it through at all, he would have realized that, even with the ability to see, he would never have had enough gas to reach the Rock.

He was going to die.

Like all creatures, he refused to accept his fate, despite the circumstances. With no way of knowing that his radio had been damaged he kept trying to contact the only person on earth who had the chance to save him.

"Sam, my faceplate has been compromised, I need help — now!"

Without knowing whether or not his flashlight had been successful in attracting Sam's attention, he switched it off. Through the millions of bubbles streaming from the crack in his faceplate, Tom saw the glowing light in the distance.

There. I have to reach it, before the darkness takes me . . .

Tom kicked his strong legs, and the fins propelled him in the direction towards the light, but without much visibility, he had little way of determining how close he was to it. Then he saw a second light, which was moving up and down, more like dolphin, towards him. And then the leaking Hydrox stopped.

He had run out of breathable gas.

Like a dying fool, Tom closed his eyes, held his breath, and swam towards his death — and death swam towards him. Within a minute, he no longer had to hold his eyes closed, and was surrounded by the darkness.

Unconsciousness wrapped itself around his mind comfortingly, like an adult spreading a warm blanket over a child.

Sam struggled to remove the deformed helmet. Using an emergency wrench connected to the back of Tom's twin dive tanks, he gripped the helmet's outer lock and pulled with all his might. The device still did not move. On his third, attempt, he got the casing to turn, then quickly pulled it off his limp friend's head.

"Tom! Can you hear me?"

Tom's eyes were open, and the man was still gasping for air, but something was wrong. The muscles around his face started to twitch.

He's been exposed to the hydrogen cyanide . . .

Opening the cyanide antidote kit, Sam said, "Matthew, put the toxicologist on the line—and I mean, right now."

Seconds later, he had a reply, "Doctor Johnston speaking."

"Tom's faceplate has been damaged and he's been exposed to high concentrations of hydrogen cyanide . . . I have the antidote kit open, but there's about ten fucking mini-jets inside—I need you to give me the sequence of administration."

"Work from left to right, for the first three. Start with the aerosol amyl nitrite—give it immediately into his mouth, and be sure to hold his nose closed."

Sam followed the order, and sprayed the aerosol solutions into Tom's mouth in rapid succession. His hands were stable. He didn't have time to be frightened. Sam now had the equipment and the instructions available. All he had to do was follow them, and Tom would survive—or he wouldn't, but he would have been given the best chance.

Without waiting for Sam to acknowledge that he'd done so, the doctor continued, "Now, on with the first injection. It's called sodium nitrite, and you're going to need to administer it intravenously. That's going to mean inserting it into Tom's large jugular vein. Make sure it's inside the vein, otherwise it won't work, and now just shove the entire contents in."

Sam had learned the basic concepts of venipuncture at college, while working on autopsies of certain mammals, but that was a far cry from inserting a massive needle into his best friend's large neck vein.

He drew on his memories, and inserted it first go.

Sam attached the mini-jet and injected the full contents. Forcing himself to take purposely slow, deep breaths, he waited for a response.

"Okay, the sodium nitrite is in."

"Good, now I want you to leave that needle inside Tom's neck and attach the second mini-jet. That one is filled with sodium thiosulfate. You will notice, it doesn't have a needle on the end. The reason for this is that you can insert it over the previous needle and just inject it straight in."

Sam followed the instructions, and then asked, "Now what?"

"If you were quick enough, and your friend is strong, he has about a 25 percent chance that he will survive. If he regains consciousness, I need you to start working through the rest of the kit—as the packet says, from left to right, each one injected through the same port that you made when you inserted the second medication into his neck vein."

"Thanks Doc," Sam said, and for an instant he thought he saw his friend's eyes starting to focus. "Now, Matthew, we only have one helmet between the two of us, and very little Hydrox in our tanks. We're going to need you to send a rescue mission."

"Rescue mission?" The incredulity in Matthew's voice could

be heard despite the radio friction. "Where the hell are you?"

"I'll explain shortly, but first, you better bring up the Rock and start preparing for a rescue mission!"

In front of him, Tom's open eyes, staring blankly into that space somewhere between life and death, appeared to recognize something. His pupils dilated, and his head turned to orient with Sam's. Without speaking, he slowly looked up, towards the glow above.

"Where the fuck are we, Sam?" Tom's voice was cold, but not frightened.

"Hey, you're alive!" Sam patted Tom's back. His friend coughed a little, but he looked like he was going to be okay. "Well Tom, I'm not certain, but if I was to hazard a guess, I'd say, we just entered the inner tomb of an ancient king."

CHAPTER 3

The air was stale, and utterly devoid of humidity.

It was the first time since entering the glowing chamber that Sam even noticed. For that matter, he was only just now able to examine his surroundings. He hadn't been aware of the unique dryness until now.

When he first dragged Tom's unresponsive body through the opening and up into the dry stone surface, Sam's only interest had been whether or not the gas was breathable. His watch monitored air quality and had quickly confirmed his suspicion that the hydrogen cyanide was confined to the water. Then he'd commenced Tom's resuscitation.

His eyes glanced over the room which now served as their rescue chamber.

It was small, no larger than someone's bedroom. The walls were built out of solid, cubed stone blocks, four feet wide. The stone walls and ceiling were entirely smooth. Above them, at the perfect center, was a square opening—just big enough for a man to climb through. It was from this opening that the strange blue glowing light radiated. Fifteen feet above, it would be nearly impossible to access without specialized equipment. Most likely, Sam guessed, this chamber served only as a deterrent for would be thieves.

His eyes returned to the walls.

Although smooth, there were a number of painted markings covering the entire chamber; pictographs which depicted warriors, with their weapons drawn as though they were placed there, ready to defend the upper levels of a vault.

Something about the pictures disturbed him.

He'd seen them somewhere before. Maybe in an archeological book or documentary on the Discovery Channel, but he doubted it. Somehow, he felt that he'd seen similar work with his own eyes. That in itself wasn't particularly surprising. After all, Sam's work with Deep Sea Expeditions, and as a ghost agent for the Secretary of Defense, often brought him to ancient archeological sites. He remembered a number of past missions that took him to Mayan sites, but failed to recall similar markings.

Without giving it any more consideration, he noticed Tom had sat up by himself, his hand instinctively reaching for the needle in his neck.

"I wouldn't touch that if I were you," Sam said.

"What is it?"

"It's a giant needle I just used to save your life."

"Do I still need it?" Tom asked.

"Probably not, but the doctors back Stateside recommended that I leave it in place, with its medical lock, until you're on the surface . . . something about an air embolism or something. How do you feel?"

"Not bad, given my recent exposure with hydrogen cyanide and concoction of otherwise lethal chemicals that you provided me with."

"You're welcome."

Tom's eyes skittered across the smashed remnants of his

dive helmet, "That's mine?"

Sam nodded his head.

Tom's hand reached for his forehead. A slight smile overcame his otherwise pensive face. "My helmet appears to have taken most of the damage."

"Yeah," Sam agreed. "Do you remember what happened?"

"Not much. I saw the light up ahead and figured it must have been your light, so I turned mine off. There must have been a crack in the outer wall, from which water was gushing at high pressure. I didn't even see it, but as I swam past, I was expelled through the water in an uncontrolled spin. My faceplate must have hit the stone, and then all I could see was the rush of Hydrox bubbles escaping my dive helmet. I knew I didn't have long to live, so when I thought I could see light in the distance, I swam towards it, hoping it was you — not that I had any idea what you could do for me. I guess somewhere along the way, my Hydrox ran out, and I succumbed to hypoxia."

"You were rambling gibberish when I got you out of the water," Sam said.

"Thank you."

"What for?"

"Saving my life — again."

Years ago, Sam had saved Tom's life on a training mission, when a $2 oil seal had failed, resulting in a total loss of oil pressure to the gearbox, and forced engine shutdown. Sam had managed to guide the helicopter into a lake and put it into a controlled descent through autorotation.

The other SEALs escaped the sinking craft, but when Sam surfaced, and a head count was performed, Tom was missing. Several of the SEALs had attempted to reach the helicopter, which had rapidly sunk to the bottom of the 80-foot lake. Sam, with his background in professional free diving, was the only one capable of reaching it. Inside, he found Tom in the cockpit, trapped by his malfunctioning seatbelt locking mechanism.

Sam laughed at the memory, as he recalled that Tom had been able to access his pilot's oxygen mask, and had been comfortably breathing the entire way to the bottom, but unable to free himself. When he'd opened the door, his friend had just looked at him, sitting comfortably in the pilot seat, as if to say, what took you so long?

"You're welcome Tom. If you count that airship last year, The Magdalena, that free dive in Saratoga, and the cave dive in Mexico when we were kids — you've still saved me more than I've saved you. I still owe you one."

"Keep it," Tom said. Then, looking around, asked, "Are you any closer to working out where we are?"

"I'm still pretty confident we're in the entrance cavity of a Mayan king's final resting chamber."

"Ajtzak's?"

"Judging from the representation of the Ark of Light at the entrance, which disappeared shortly before Ajtzak's death, I think there's a good chance this is it."

"What about our rescue team — do you think we'll make it until they can reach us?"

"The air's dry, but the quality is surprisingly good. We have plenty of time. Matthew will get us out of here — don't you worry. It will take them another hour for the rescue team to reach us," Sam cast his eyes around the cavern. "Care to take a look around?"

Sam examined the opening in the ceiling above.

It was ten feet above them and perfectly square, with smooth edges of cut rock. When he was younger and played basketball at college, he could easily have jumped high enough to touch it. But he needed more than that. He needed to be able to climb into it, and once there, he would have to find a way to climb up the vertical shaft.

"You feeling strong Tom?"

"Strong enough — what have you got in mind?"

"I was thinking if I could stand on your shoulders, I might just be able to reach high enough into the opening to climb it."

"I can get you up to it, but I haven't a clue how you plan to climb it once you get there," Tom replied.

"Leave that to me."

Tom stood up, his entire six feet five inches making the challenge seem less daunting. He was tall and lanky, but his muscles were misleading, and he was probably the naturally strongest man Sam had ever met.

"You okay?" Sam checked again before climbing the monster of a man.

"I'll be fine."

Tom took a firm stance with his feet square to his giant shoulders and his arms in the air.

"Count of three?"

"Sure."

"One . . . Two . . . Three . . ." Sam climbed up Tom's back as though it were a tree stump. It was strong and hard as one, too.

Standing firmly on top of Tom's shoulders, he was now able to reach the entrance. The stone walls inside the shaft were smooth like those below, making any thoughts of climbing next

37

to impossible. Sam calmly withdrew a small metal device from his pocket. It looked very much like a flashlight. He placed it horizontally inside the opening and then pressed a green button. The device opened wider as its hydraulics moved outwards, until it became firmly lodged between the stone walls.

Sam then placed a second one just a little higher, and then gripping the higher of the two rods, he lifted his feet on top of the first and swung himself up. Once standing fully on the first bar, Sam was easily able to reach the top of the vertical tunnel.

"What did I say? Easy . . ." Sam gloated.

"Cheat." Tom looked at him from below. "Am I coming with you?"

Sam then unrolled a small, nylon ladder. It was attached to the second rod, which he'd fixed to the very top of the vertical opening.

"Come on up."

The second chamber appeared to be identical to the first, only this one had giant statues on either side of the opening. One at each end, both stood at least seven feet high. It was impossible to determine if they were supposed to be enemies or friends—both were fully clad in warrior garments.

"Do you think one of these guys is Ajtzak?" Tom asked.

"Could be. I've never seen a picture of him."

Directly above the opening through which Sam had entered the chamber was another shaft extending high above them.

Sam took a step back to examine the place, and felt the block below his foot move slightly. Below, a sound of high pressured liquid moving stone, could be heard.

He looked around the room, half expecting the walls to cave in on him, "Any ideas where they came from Tom?"

"I heard it, but I can't see anything."

Sam bent down to disconnect his hydraulic device from the shaft below.

"Say Tom, did you happen to notice those spears there on our way up?"

"What spears?"

Tom looked down the shaft they had just climbed.

Four large spears, made of iron, had appeared from the floor below.

"Whoever built this didn't plan on any grave robbers," Sam said.

"Yeah, well I have no desire to rob from the dead, but do you have a plan to get out of here?"

"Not yet. I'm working on it." Sam then looked around the room and at the shaft above. "Shall we continue?"

"After you."

Sam followed the same plan as the first one they had used to reach the next chamber. The only difference was that this time the stakes had lethal consequences if he failed.

Sam climbed the stone ladder nearly seventy feet before he came to the final chamber. His head had barely passed the opening, and he was certain that they had discovered the final resting place of a king, *but which king?*

Tom popped his head up through the shaft a moment latter.

"I'll be darned!"

"What is it, Tom?"

"We've just found the final resting place of king Ajtzak."

At the center of the room, directly above the shaft that ran all the way to the entrance of the pyramid's chambers more than a hundred feet below, Tom was able to see the source of the strange bluish glow. A perfectly round ball, no larger than his fist and made of a dark blue crystal-like stone, resonated light, as though it were a diamond.

Where it drew its light from remained a mystery — Tom could only guess. The Mayans who had built it had somehow drawn light from hundreds of feet above, perhaps so it would always shine on their old king.

It must still be daytime outside.

The room was large, maybe forty feet wide. Its walls rose in a perfect pyramid, culminating in the roof high above and meeting where the blue stone rested, like a world globe illuminating the room. At each of the four walls, a single man stood with his hands above his head as though he were supporting the roof above. There, more than a hundred intricate pictographs and hieroglyphics adorned the room.

At the center of the room, a sarcophagus rested.

On top of it, a pictograph depicted a man holding a scepter. Only, the man was garlanded in colorful stones, and the scepter was formed by an indentation on the sarcophagus, as though the real scepter awaited to be returned.

"What makes you so certain this was king Ajtzak's tomb?" Sam interrupted his examination of the room.

"Because that's his family emblem."

"What is?"

Tom touched the pictograph at the base of the sarcophagus, "Here. See these four horsemen, carrying spears? They're looking up and worshiping their deity — a man with a hawk head and headdress with a sun disk."

"AKA, Ra, the Sun God in ancient Egyptian culture," Sam stared at it in wonder.

"Right you are. Hey, what do you know about Egypt?"

"You'd be surprised."

Tom ran his hands along the crest of the deity, and then added, "I only remember it because when I called a professor of Mayan archaeology at the University of Mexico, he said that Ajtzak used a very specific symbol, which looked almost exactly like that of Ra, the God of Sun. But, as even I know, the mention of Ra was only ever found in Egypt, never on this side of the Atlantic. What's stranger still, this reference to Ra, can't be found anywhere else throughout his bloodline or the rest of the Mayan culture."

"The Egyptians believed that Ra was swallowed every night by the sky goddess Nut, and was reborn every morning. They also believed that he traveled through the underworld at night," Sam repeated what he knew about Ra.

"So the real question to ask is, what is an Egyptian sized pyramid and Egyptian God doing on this side of the Atlantic, at the burial site for a Mayan King?"

"I have no idea. But if we can get this cyanide problem fixed, I'm sure some archeologists are going to have a field day in here." Sam regarded the walls again. "I had a quick look at Mayan mythology on my tablet while waiting for you to come round earlier. It appears this room is an abstract combination of the Mayan beliefs."

"Such as?"

"The Maya believe in a universe consisting of heavens above and underworlds below, with the human world between. Linking the three realms was a giant tree whose roots reached into the underworld and branches stretched to heaven. The gods and the souls of the dead traveled between worlds along

41

this tree."

"Interesting. So we've just found the inner sanctum of king Ajtzak's tomb?" Tom tapped on the sarcophagus. "Are you starting to get the feeling that no one really knew this king? As though, maybe, he came from somewhere else?"

"As in, Egypt?" Sam replied.

"Exactly."

Tom continued to scan the vivid imagery on the walls. There were animals and humans, snakes — all sorts of creatures. Tunnels, similar to the shafts he had just climbed, appeared to swirl around the walls of the room, until he realized that they weren't tunnels — they were branches of a tree, and its roots.

On the wall was a symbol Tom had never seen before. It was small, and made of bronze, depicting a man with a measuring tool standing above an army. It seemed almost irrelevant compared with the other treasures that adorned the King's final resting chamber. Yet somehow, it looked like it could have once been important.

One look at Sam's face when he saw it confirmed his instincts.

"You've seen it before?"

"Yes." Sam was quiet and unusually distant.

"Where?" Tom pursued the question. It was unlike Sam to be coy with him. "What does it mean?"

"Back in Afghanistan . . . When I was removed from active duty, I was sent to explore a prehistoric ruin, overrun with encryptions and mazes. At the very top of the structure was the symbol of the civilization that built it. Their mark. It was simple, almost bland by comparison with the structure they had created — just like that one . . ."

"So, you're saying that these people, who lived in

Afghanistan many years ago, also lived in Central America?"

"No."

"But this is the tomb of a Mayan King?"

"Yes, but the Master Builders lived by building great structures. One theory is that they never even built these things themselves, but instead commanded great armies to do it for them. They would have been more accurately described as Master Engineers. And this, I believe, would have been just one of their many projects—for a price."

"And what was that price?"

"That I've never been able to work out. In fact, so far, I don't even have proof they ever existed. The only evidence I have is that many of the ancient wonders could not have been built without such a race."

Eight hours later, after a prolonged decompression period in the Rock, Sam and Tom stepped outside the hyperbaric chamber and onto the deck of the moon pool. Sam looked at the faces of the people who worked and lived aboard the Maria Helena. They were his family, and each face displayed its own way of coping with a near death experience of one of its members.

"All right, you lot. We're okay." Sam scanned their faces for relief, and found none. "We all know it takes a lot more than a cracked faceplate at a few hundred feet of water to damage Tom's ugly face any more than Mother Nature."

"I've had a look myself, and I think the blow might have done some improvements." Tom spoke with the relaxed self-assurance of a man whose strong jaw line and intensely grey, piercing eyes, had stolen many a woman's heart.

"Now, as much as I'm glad you all care about our survival, we have some important work ahead of us. Let's not forget that several tons of hydrogen cyanide are still leaking out of a hole in the seafloor. I want everyone in the mission room within ten minutes. Grab yourselves a quick coffee, or whatever drug you use to keep focused. I need to debrief what we discovered, and plan our next steps."

Eight minutes later, Sam stood at the head of the table in the mission room. Each person on board the Maria Helena was there, all fifteen of them, and each looked up, focused on what he was about to say. He could feel the tension as he spoke.

"We made our dive to the seafloor in search of one answer, but have instead come back with a multitude of unanswered questions. Two distinctly different challenges, requiring two different teams to resolve. The first, and paramount purpose of our mission is to discover the source of the leaking hydrogen cyanide and block it. The second is of an archeological nature. The pyramid will be treated as an archeological site, with our team primarily providing the logistical needs of the archeologists to investigate."

Sam drank from his cup of hot chocolate before he continued speaking. "It appears that the source of the hydrogen cyanide leak is through a crack in the outer wall of a subterranean Mayan pyramid. It's unlikely to have come from the local silver mine as first expected, but instead from a cyanide store."

"Mayan cyanide store?" Veyron asked.

"Yes, Mayan. I do realize that cyanide wasn't utilized in mining until the 17th century in Europe, but there has been evidence over the years that both the Mayans and the Aztecs discovered the benefit cyanide served in separating raw mining materials such as gold and silver, centuries earlier. My guess is that a recent drilling or explosions from the nearby silver mine most likely damaged the old store, sending its lethal poison into the Gulf."

"I want you, Veyron, to head up a team of engineers to work out the solution to remove any additional poison from the cracked wall. Then work out a way to fill the entire area with concrete, so that if we miss anything, it will be another thousand years before the stuff escapes again."

"Got it," Veyron acknowledged.

"Tom, once someone checks you out and makes certain you're fit to dive again, I want you to head up a team to search the pyramid and what appeared to be the King's Tomb."

"You don't want to run it?" Tom asked, his surprise clearly evident in his face.

"I do, but my first mission must be to resolve this marine catastrophe." Sam grinned. "I have a number of personal reasons why I'm intent on exploring the pyramid's hidden secrets, but it can't be my priority. I'm going to need to make some calls, and manage the overall project from topside. Don't forget, we have less than a month until we're in the midst of hurricane season. It might sound straightforward, but don't forget we're working in up to 400 feet of water, inside a narrow tunnel. We have no way of knowing how stable the pyramid's walls are, or what's on the other side of that cracked wall."

Veyron raised his left hand, only slightly, as though he had something to say.

"Yes, Veyron?"

"Why don't we just back fill the entire pyramid with concrete? It would be less risky, and I'm sure whoever's buried down there wouldn't mind being just that little bit more . . . how do I say? Snug?"

"We may have to if our first option becomes too difficult or unsafe, but I believe this site holds far too many secrets and insights into the Mayan culture to be forever buried in thousands of tons of concrete. During the Spanish conquest, the Catholic Church and colonial officials, guided by Bishop Diego de Landa, destroyed Maya texts wherever they found them, and with them the knowledge of Maya writing. The writings on these walls may hold a wealth of information about pre-Spanish Mayan culture, which I would hate to see buried for eternity."

"Okay, I'll do my best to preserve it," Veyron acknowledged.

Returning to the cyanide problem, Sam continued, "For all we know, the mine has been stockpiling the waste product from their silver mine in an underground tunnel, with no idea that one day it would break into a pyramid. Make no mistake ladies and gentlemen, this is a serious undertaking, with deadly consequences for the world's marine life."

Veyron said, "Regardless of who owned the cyanide once upon a time, I believe it is safe to say that the silver mine is somehow responsible for the damage that caused the leak. And if they have been dumping cyanide for years, we better know now rather than later, before we drill into something that we shouldn't."

"Good thinking," Sam said. "If I know big mining, they're going to drag this thing on through every loophole possible until the EPA forces their hand. It's going to be nasty, but I'll make the call. TRY and get hold of the owner, Michael Rodriguez, first, and see if we can get around some of the red tape."

Tom grinned mischievously, "I don't think that will be necessary."

"Why's that?"

"Because I think that's his helicopter approaching now."

CHAPTER 4

Michael Rodriguez flew into Mexico that morning on his private jet. It was hot, but unlike Spain, which enjoyed the cool breeze off the Adriatic Sea at the entrance to the Med, Mexico always seemed dry. It was one of his least favorite mines, but there was no avoiding it today.

Nothing ever happened without his knowledge — on any one of his 43 prized mineral mines. He was an owner who maintained a very active control of the day to day workings of each of his mines, and prided himself on his ability to ensure their efficiency and the loyalty of his employees.

Rodriguez Mining Inc. was started by his grandfather in 1928. Originally, a single gold mine in South Africa, which he'd bought after luck granted him a relative fortune with the discovery of the Royal Clipper, an 80-ounce gold nugget. As the world turned to ruin and the great depression struck solid in 1930, he bought up a number of mines at prices below the value of their inventory. It was a gamble that paid huge dividends in the lead up to the Second World War in 1939, when Germany began stockpiling gold and iron ore.

By the time Michael's father took over in 1962, the company was already rich. But by embracing the newer drilling technology, he drove the company to be one of the most profitable mining conglomerates in the world, with mines on every continent.

History teaches us that the first generation of entrepreneurs make the money, the second improve on that money, and the third—loses it all. If, somehow, the third generation manages to keep the wealth inside the family from becoming lost in gluttony, greed and temptation, then the family often goes on to being generational old money, such as the Rothschilds, the Waltons, or the Arnaults of the world. The families entire nations borrowed money from.

It was his plan, among others, to place the name of Rodriguez beside those names of the uppermost echelon of rich.

He had flown in immediately when he heard that the Maria Helena was snooping near his mine. He had a fair idea what they were after. It had been all over the world news that the Dead Zone had increased since last year by a factor of nearly 100.

Michael couldn't have cared less about the environmental losses, but where unexplained environmental accidents occur, local mines often got the blame. No, he would have to show a presence at the investigation if he wanted to keep Rodriguez Mining Inc. above board. It was a small price to pay for what he wanted in the long run.

His private jet had just stopped rolling on the tarmac at Mexico's Ciudad Del Carmen International Airport, when he stepped off it and boarded a company helicopter. The best way, he decided, to keep things in his favor, was to meet the crew of the Maria Helena in person.

Immediately, before they sought him.

Within twenty minutes, the company helicopter landed on the rear deck, next to another helicopter on board the Maria Helena. While the rotors slowed, Michael, not prone to waiting for anything, stepped out and walked towards the crew behind the decking—where the man who held the outcome of all his dreams, stood waiting for him.

Sam watched the stranger approach.

He was maybe ten years Sam's senior, but bounded out the helicopter like a much younger man, paying no attention to the spinning rotary blades above his head. It was a sign he was confident around helicopters, or lived in such a world that he believed himself above the possibility of harm. His height was average, and although approaching his mid-forties, Sam guessed, his athletic stride and upright posture displayed the remnants of someone who had once been a boxer. And none of the usual signs of someone who'd inherited nearly 25 billion dollars, such as a team of bodyguards, or flab from a lifetime of inactivity and excess.

"Good morning. Which one of you is Sam Reilly?" he asked, holding out his hand. The man wore a confident smile, and spoke like a man who was used to being listened to. Despite his Spanish origins, he spoke perfect English. His voice betrayed a very slight trace of a Boston accent—the latter being most likely the result of his Harvard education.

"That would be me," Sam said, meeting him half way to shake hands.

The man met Sam's eyes immediately. "My name is Michael Rodriguez."

"Pleased to meet you, Mr. Rodriguez."

"Call me Mick . . ." Smiling affably, he winked and said, "Only my employees and those who want to suck up to me for money call me Mr. Rodriguez. Unless, that is, you want to work for me? Because I know you don't need the money."

So he knows who I am . . . or at least who my father is . . .

"Sure." Sam was surprised by Mick's gregarious attitude. Growing up with his own father, he had met many of the world's ultra-rich, and this man made the first exception to the rule, that all such men act as if and believe they own the planet and all those within it. "What can I do for you, Mick?"

"Sam . . . may I call you Sam?" Mick asked and then, receiving the slight nod from Sam, continued, "I've heard reports that record numbers of fish have been found dead or dying near "The Dipper," one of my silver mines. Each year the Dead Zone seems to be getting worse . . . maybe there's something to this whole global warming thing, or maybe we just take too much from the soil through Northern America?"

Sam wasn't sure whether or not Mick was attacking America's stance on global warming. He was about to mention that this year's cause of the Dead Zone was triggered by the mine, when Mick continued to speak.

"I'm here to say that I would like to offer you our full support with your investigation."

"That's very good of you, Mick."

"Not at all. It's the least someone born into my position could offer. Do we have any idea what's been causing it?"

"As a matter of fact, we do," Sam said.

"Well, don't leave me in suspense, son, what's causing this disaster?"

"It appears that blasting from your mine may have caused damage to a local Mayan tomb site of great archeological significance, which has in turn released large amounts of hydrogen cyanide into the waters."

"Cyanide? We don't even use that on our mine site. We're a silver mine, not a gold mine — I've no idea where that could have even come from."

"We don't know for certain yet, but it appears the Mayans may have discovered the benefits of cyanide in separating gold many centuries before the Europeans did back in the seventeenth century. Somehow, your blasting appears to have opened an old Mayan stockpile."

"Okay, wow. So what can we do about it?"

"We're going to need to send a team in to find the primary source of contamination. Then, we're going to need to safely secure it without damaging the archeological site, which will be performed by another team in conjunction with the Mexican government. Last, we're going to need to repopulate the local fish."

"Not a problem, pal. Let me know what assistance you need, and I'll give you my full support. Then send me the bill. If we caused this mess, I want to take responsibility for it. We're not one of those companies that destroys the land and then moves on without repairing."

"That's very good of you, Mick. You'll be the first I've had dealings with to take responsibility with such equanimity. We appreciate it."

"Not a problem. I still don't know how this could have been caused by one of my blasting sites. I mean, it's very unlikely that the aftershock could have damaged the Ciudad Del Carmen," Mick said, his voice confident, but not pugnacious. "Roberto Jackson, my manager of the mine, says that the Little Dipper has gone to great lengths to protect the valuable archeological relics of Ciudad Del Carmen. In fact, I made the decision a couple of years ago to halt tunneling down the southern long wall, because of the low level risk. Now, the mine moves more towards the north and east, well below the ocean floor."

"I know it does."

"Then why do you believe that it's my mine that has caused all this damage?"

"Because it wasn't the Ciudad Del Carmen that was damaged."

The skin around Mick's strong jawline tightened — only slightly, but it was the first time Sam had noticed the man's confidence waver. He was probably only just now realizing that it was possible for his mine to be responsible for a disaster that may end up costing him millions to repair.

"Then what Mayan archeological site were you referring to? There aren't any other sites nearby." His eyebrow rose with genuine curiosity.

"A subterranean pyramid, found beneath the ocean seabed . . ." Sam pointed on a map of the Gulf of Mexico to the exact location, "right here."

"Shit." Rodriguez' face became ashen, and small drops of sweat dripped from his forehead despite the Maria Helena's powerful air conditioning. "That's exactly where the Big Dipper runs!"

Sam hadn't considered the significance until that moment. "If it breaks through, more than 400 feet of water will be pushed through at a force that will kill everyone inside the tunnel!"

"Exactly . . . please forgive me for a moment, I must call my underground manager."

"Of course."

Sam watched as Rodriguez calmly walked towards the outer deck, where his helicopter now rested silently. The man spoke on the phone for a couple minutes. His legs were firm on the deck, not pacing, like so many do during a crisis.

"What do you make of him?" Tom asked.

"I don't know yet. He seems like a nice enough guy, for someone who's on the same playing field as my father in overall wealth, but there's something that I don't trust about him. I just don't know what . . . maybe it's just my inbuilt dislike of the ultra-rich."

"Yeah, I hate you rich guys, too . . ."

"It's nothing that he's done or said. It's what he hasn't that concerns me."

"What do you mean? He sounded to me like he was happy to provide whatever help he could."

"That's just it. Do you know what my dad's response was when I told him what the Maria Helena was spending her time doing this month?"

"No."

"He said, 'but there can't be much money in that sort of work.' That's what people in my dad's caliber like to do. Avoid paying what they owe. This man sounds like he hasn't even talked to his lawyers yet, despite potentially being liable for millions."

"Okay, I'll keep my eyes on him. See what wildcard he thinks he's holding up his sleeve."

Mick walked back, the serious look on his face now gone. "I'm sorry about that. I just called my underground manager. He's pulling the team out of the tunnel now. I've more than a thousand Mexican workers several hundred feet below the waterline. If that thing breaks, every one of them will be dead before they know what hit them. We're going to have to send a team through to close the entire tunnel, or risk killing them all. The biggest problem is that water is coming through small cracks, and there's a practical river pouring down the tunnel. The pumps should be able to keep the tunnels open to my men, but the flowing water will make it very difficult to reach."

"With that, I might just have a solution . . ." Sam said.

Sam switched on the projector.

It showed a hand-drawn diagram of the subterranean Mayan pyramid. A red symbol like a lightning bolt highlighted the point on the eastern tunnel of the pyramid where Tom had been nearly killed by the outward flowing hydrogen cyanide.

"This is where the crack was found in the tunnel." Sam pointed to the spot where the leak was first identified. "We'll have no way of finding out how close the other side of the hole is to the Big Dipper, but for the blasting at that point to damage the enormous blocks, one must assume that it's pretty close."

Mick opened up his computer tablet. "Here's the schematics of the Big Dipper. Our tunnel draws directly below the subterranean pyramid — about ten feet below. For our blasting to cause that type of damage between the two structures, there would have to be an opening somewhere already."

"Perhaps the Mayans maintained a storeroom underneath the pyramid that we would be able to see?" Mick asked.

"It's highly possible," Sam accepted. "So, you were considering sending in a team of miners, who would be willing to take the risk of entering the mine and blasting the roof in from about 50 feet below the pyramid?"

"Yes."

"Mick, you pointed out that the risk would be high, and failure would result in the flooding of your entire mine." Sam saw Mick nod in agreement and then, pointing to the diagram of the pyramid, asked, "What if we blocked the entrance to the pyramid here, and here?"

"Then, the pyramid would remain lost forever?" Mick asked.

"No, then your team could go in and seal the mine from below, losing no more than 50 feet of your long wall. Once that was complete, we would remain with a team of archeologists to remove the blocked entrance and explore the Mayan tomb."

"How soon can you do it?" Mick asked, his eyes wide with respect.

Tom looked at his engineer, "Veyron — what do you think?"

"I need to build the steel framework and then pump the concrete. Ideally, I'll need about three days, given the location."

Sam looked back at Mick to see if that would meet his new friend's approval.

It looked like Mick hadn't heard it. Instead he was speaking on his cell phone, his body tense with anxiety. "I understand. Do what you can — pull everyone out."

"What's happened?" Sam asked.

"That was my underground manager. The water's just burst through the tunnel."

"Shit. Okay, at least you got your workers out . . ."

"That's just it though . . . my underground manager just told me he pulled them from the Big Dipper, and moved them to Mine Shaft Four. He thought it would be safe there, because of the twenty miles between the two shafts. But that amount of water will fill that distance quick."

"Okay, how long do we have?"

"Maybe an hour, at best."

"Can't he just pull them out now?"

"No, the entrance is blocked by the oncoming water. They're trapped literally below the torrent of water."

"He thought he'd move them to safety, by mining below the water line?" Sam said, with no attempt to hide the contempt from his voice.

"Mining is expensive. He was just trying to maintain production." Michael spoke honestly, and without shame. It was obvious that mining was a hard man's game. "Now, what are we able to do about it?"

Sam looked at Veyron again.

"It will break my heart, Sam, but we could use the Sea Witch to block the entrance to the pyramid. Her solid steel hull would plug the entrance."

"Do it." Sam said, without another thought for the destruction of his 5-million-dollar machine.

Tom climbed down the reinforced steel hatch, and into Sea Witch's cockpit.

In the pilot seat, Sam sat, already commencing the startup procedure. Behind him, Veyron was going over a final check of the submarine. Next to Veyron rested a single piece of scrap paper — on top of which, a number of algorithms and mathematical equations were scribbled in careless handwriting.

Ordinarily, he would trust the man's calculations with the confidence that came by working with an expert, but on a complex dive like this, they might usually have weeks of preparation. Today's mission was determined out of necessity, after discovering they had less than an hour to save the lives of more than 1000 people.

The cable and hooks were attached to the submarine, ready for launch. Tom felt the sub shift as he strapped himself into the copilot seat.

"Well gentlemen, I guess that's my cue," Veyron said. "This is where I get off."

"Thanks, Veyron," Sam said without looking up from the instruments he was checking.

"Hey Veyron." Tom stopped him, for a second.

"Yeah?"

"How confident are you that this crazy scheme's going to work?"

"That the Sea Witch will block the entrance to the pyramid?" Veyron frowned, narrowed his eyes and glanced up and to the left. He appeared to be performing mental arithmetic. "I'd say, at least 95%."

"That's sounds all right."

"But that the structure of the Sea Witch will maintain its ability to withhold the pressure, and you aren't crushed to death? I'd say, definitely better than 50:50." Without waiting for Tom's response, he then climbed the last rungs of the ladder, and said, "Best of luck, gentlemen."

"Thanks for the vote of confidence," Tom replied.

Sam grinned. "Those odds aren't too bad. Tom and I have survived worse.

Above, Veyron closed the first hatch. The ratcheting, grinding sound of the mechanical locking mechanism being engaged echoed in Sam's ears as its twelve hydraulic locks slid into place. The first red flashing light turned to green.

Tom started work on his safety check sheet. As the submarine shifted under the crane's steel wire, swinging mildly, he lurched but didn't let the movement distract him.

Above, the second light switched green — confirming that the airlock and outer hatch were both sealed.

"Maria Helena, this is Sea Witch, ready for launch." Sam's voice was slow and confident, as though he were on any other mission.

"Sea Witch, we're commencing lowering now." Tom could hear the concern in Matthew's otherwise controlled voice. He was glad that Sam had left Matthew in charge of the mission room — not that he was in a position to help them if something went wrong.

The motorized winch crank could be heard gently running out the cable until the Sea Witch reached the moon pool's surface. The left porthole disappeared under the splashing water, and then the Sea Witch started to float.

Sam turned on each of the propellers, confirming that she was ready to maneuver herself, and then said, "Maria Helena, we're ready to disengage."

"Copy, Sea Witch, disengaging now."

They took one last glance topside through the small porthole, which allowed the submarine's occupants to observe the attachment of the crane's cables. Tom saw Veyron, thumbs up, giving the all clear sign.

"Sea Witch, you're clear. Best of luck."

Sam arched an eyebrow. "You ready, Tom?"

"Yep, let's do this."

Sam flooded the main diving chambers. Immediately the Sea Witch began sinking.

Tom looked at Sam, who was now whistling, as the submarine dived, and said, "So, 50:50 chance we don't get crushed to death before we exit the escape hatch, hey? How do you feel about those odds?"

Sam grinned and Tom shook his head. Sam was giving him that damn demonic smile, the smile of a madman about to do something stupid and try to get away with it. But in Sam's case, he usually did.

"Listen here, Tom, and I'll tell you exactly how we're going to pull this off."

Michael answered the phone.

"Yes?"

"Mr. Rodriguez, the water has reached mine shaft number two and it's already starting to overflow into three!" His underground manager sounded out of breath. "Once it reaches number four, there's nothing we can do for the men below."

"Reilly's in the water. They should have the hole blocked within the next 45 minutes . . ."

"And if they don't succeed in the next thirty, about 1000 miners are going to die."

"Understood, Roberto."

The briefest of smiles curled on Michael's lips as he reflected on the wonder of human nature.

Fascinating how my underground manager beat the odds and reached the surface, despite sending the rest of the men to work further below the waterline.

Sam could see the entrance of the pyramid up ahead on the sonar screen.

Tom, who was now in control of the submarine, slowed to a crawl and asked, "Okay, it's 40 feet ahead. Are you going to share your plan with me any time soon, Sam?"

Sam attached his dive belt.

"All right. Now's probably as good a time as any. Basically, the plan, as discussed with Veyron, was that we would take Sea Witch close to the entrance of the pyramid until its massive pull sucks us in towards the main point where the tunnel narrows, just before splitting in two. Thus, we're going to block the entrance, as a plug would a bathtub."

"That much I already knew."

"Good to see you were awake." Sam handed Tom his new dive helmet. "Veyron's done the math, and the Sea Witch will survive being used as a giant plug. What he wasn't certain about was whether or not the sub would then implode after it had been weakened by the initial force of striking the wall as it blocked the entrance to the pyramid."

"Right . . . yeah, he said he gave us about a 50:50 chance of implosion."

"Based on calculations of our hull already being completely airtight, and then we would escape through the escape hatch, return to the diving bell, having achieved our mission . . ." Sam looked up, and, reassured that Tom was following, said, "But what if the Sea Witch was already flooded?"

"You want to flood the interior of the sub?"

"Sure, why not? It's going to be wrecked after this anyway." Sam's face showed genuine disinterest.

"The power will short out the instant the main chamber becomes flooded, and we won't be able to maneuver it."

"That shouldn't be a problem. After all, it's going to be dragged in by the undercurrent anyway. Then, instead of imploding, it should just lodge itself in the opening. Probably . . ." Sam mused with a fatalistic grin. "Why, have you got a better idea?"

"No . . . I don't. So I guess we're all out of options."

Sam turned the dive tanks to on, and locked his dive helmet.

"You ready?"

"No, but we don't have much choice," Tom replied, checking his Hydrox intake to his helmet.

"Here we go."

Sam brought the Sea Witch slowly closer to the main entrance of the pyramid, until he noticed some of the controls were becoming soft and awkward. He still had control over the sub, but needed to exert more pressure to achieve it.

"Okay, that's it," Sam said. "We're committed now."

"Copy that. Overriding the airlock's primary hatch."

The outside hatch remained firmly closed, while the middle hatch, which ordinarily ensured that the sub's cockpit remained dry, stayed opened. There were a number of safety systems in place to avoid just such an event, but Tom had managed to override them.

"Flooding her now," Tom said.

Water quickly filled both chambers of the Sea Witch.

By the time they reached the entrance to the pyramid, the sub was completely flooded, and the pressure equalized with the outside environment.

Without power, the Sea Witch spun through the turbid waters.

Looking out the tiny porthole, Sam struggled to maintain a sense of direction as they bounced through the large entrance to the pyramid. Unable to determine how far along the tunnel they had reached, the sub suddenly jerked to a standstill and became firmly lodged.

"Are we stuck?" Tom asked.

Sam looked out his porthole. Water appeared to be flowing

past it, faster and angrier than ever. "Yeah, we're stuck all right, but not where we were supposed to be."

Tom ran his hand over his dive computer. All the instruments were working, and at this depth, he had a little more than an hour's Hydrox supply — that was something, at least.

"How's your Hydrox, Sam?"

"I'm good for at least an hour. Let's open the hatch and get back to the diving bell. See what our next move is."

"Agreed."

Tom spun the internal locking wheel of the outer hatch. The green light turned red, indicating that it was no longer water tight.

He then pushed the door outwards.

Nothing happened.

He pushed at it again, without any success. Tom swallowed and his heart rate rocketed. "Sam, we have a big problem . . ."

In the mission room of the Maria Helena, the silent uneasiness was almost tangible. Sam's last message from the Sea Witch was that they had flooded the cockpit and were now drifting inside the mouth of the pyramid. The last five minutes had passed unbearably slowly, and they had received no messages from below.

The sound of Michael's cell ringing, broke the silence.

"The water's still flowing, and it's passed the safety blocks at mineshaft three!" It was his underground manager.

"Understood. Tell the men that we're doing our best for them."

Michael looked at Matthew. "It didn't work. The water's still flowing strong."

Matthew nodded in understanding and then looked at Veyron, "Any ideas?"

"None that can be done in the timeframe, I'm afraid."

"Veyron," Michael said. "I noticed you have a second submarine down below. Can you send that to try again?"

"Sure, I can control its mechanical arms and probably reposition the Sea Witch, but we don't have anyone to pilot her."

"I think I've got a solution for that."

CHAPTER 5

Sam turned around so that he could push the hatch with his legs, in conjunction with Tom. Despite the pain in his strong thigh muscles, there was no movement.

"Well . . . that's going to make our day considerably worse," Sam said.

Tom moved around the sub, looking out the other portholes, trying to get a better idea of how the Sea Witch was resting. "The hatch must be wedged up against the wall?"

"I suppose so. The question is how are we going to free it?"

"I'll inform the Maria Helena that we failed, and see what solutions Veyron can come up with. I knew we should have taken that French son of a bitch with us."

Sam nodded his head and then continued his reconnaissance of the Sea Witch. It appeared to be lying with a 70-degree list to its portside, meaning that the hatch—the only place of exit—was wedged between the submarine and the granite walls of the pyramid's tunnel. The seawater had completely shorted all electrical systems inside the sub.

He looked at his dive computer.

It showed 55 minutes of Hydrox remaining.

They were now trapped inside the flooded safest deep sea submarine in existence, with less than an hour remaining of breathable gas, and no means of escape.

"Our luck doesn't seem to be getting much better," Tom said.

"Let me guess. We lost the radio transmitter from the top of the sub?"

"Yep," Tom confirmed. "It's just that sort of day, isn't it? So, now we're trapped, and we have no means of communicating with the Maria Helena. Not that it matters much. They have no one to pilot Rescue One down here in the time we need."

Sam unlocked the storage locker on the side, which would ordinarily be at the bottom of the sub, pulling out a tool kit. "Okay, so we're on our own." His voice appeared content, as though he'd calmly accepted their predicament.

"Seems like it."

Sam removed several items from the tool kit, discarding them on the floor with disinterest.

"What are you after?" Tom asked.

"A hyperbaric blowtorch."

"Are you kidding me, Sam? The steel in this sub is eight inches thick. You would most likely starve to death before you managed to burn a hole through it."

"You're right," Sam agreed, and then switched the blowtorch on and off again. "But I've no desire to burn my way out."

"What then?"

"We're jammed up against the hatch on one side, and the mechanical robot arms on the other side." Sam looked at Tom, to make sure that he was following. "I'm going to cut the hydraulic lines to those arms."

"Detaching the wedge, and sending the Sea Witch spiraling down the tunnel again."

Sam removed the protective cover to the starboard side wall, where he could see the robotic arms were resting firmly on the granite walls of the pyramid's tunnel. Three hydraulic lines ran along the barren submarine's inner surface.

"That's the plan. The question is, where are we going to end up, this time?"

"There's only one way to find out," Tom replied.

Sam switched the hyperbaric blowtorch on. Its blue flame hissed out of the end of the nozzle. Cutting the tough hydraulic wires like butter, he started at the top.

"One at a time, Sam. It will give us more of a chance to move just enough to escape."

"Good idea."

The first hydraulic strut did nothing.

Out the porthole, Sam could see the limp arm of one of the robots that hadn't been trapped on the side of the tunnel.

The second one was connected to the largest of the five robotic arms, which appeared to be wedged and responsible for their problem.

Sam cut it and watched a plume of black oil spurt out under pressure.

He then looked out the porthole.

The arm had not moved at all.

Sam looked at his watch. He now had 25 minutes of Hydrox left to breathe. "Any idea why that didn't take the pressure off that arm?"

"No."

Sam proceeded to cut the fifth and final hydraulic strut. "Lucky last."

Nothing happened.

Peering out the porthole, Sam noticed the robotic arm appeared as inflexible as ever.

"Now we're in trouble," Tom said.

"I don't know what's keeping it rigid. I've cut the strut. Look at it, it's still pissing out oil."

"Of course!" Tom braced himself against the submarine wall. "The pressure hasn't fully left the strut–"

The robotic arm retracted with a violent CRASH!

Sam grabbed hold of a bracing bar, just in time for the submarine to start spinning again. They went circling down the tunnel, as though they were being flushed down a toilet bowl.

It rolled nearly a dozen times before finally coming to rest.

Sam stared out the porthole.

The murky water appeared to be slowing down, as though something was impeding its movement. Whatever water was making its way through, it wouldn't be enough to drown the miners below. On the other side of the submarine, Sam could see Tom taking a long look out the other side.

"The water's stopped!" Tom said.

Sam looked at the position of the hatch, now below his feet. "That's great, but I think we're now resting right on top of the hatch."

At the pilot controls of the submarine, Rescue One, Michael watched the sudden movement of the Sea Witch in horror. Something appeared to have given way, so that the small submarine started tumbling down the tunnel again.

"What the hell happened?" he asked.

"If I had a guess, I'd say Sam just worked out how to cut the hydraulic cables for the robotic arm, freeing the Sea Witch to be drawn further down the tunnel," Veyron replied.

"That's great."

"It may be. And it might not."

"What do you mean? Why not?"

Veyron adjusted the angle of his sonar, and said, "Unless they had the good fortune to land in such a way that they block the tunnel and also have access to their hatch, we're going to have to go in there after them."

"And, did they have good luck?"

"How's the current? Is Rescue One still pulling towards the entrance?"

"Yes, but it's not as strong," Michael confirmed.

Next to him, Veyron pulled away from the sonar screen. "Shit."

"It's not where it needs to be?"

"No. As luck would have it, the Sea Witch appears to be lying upside down, which means there's no possible way they can get out." Veyron looked at his watch. "And by my calculations, they don't have much more Hydrox to breathe. You'd better take us in."

"You want me to navigate Rescue One, in there?" Michael was incredulous.

"I believe it is the only way we can move the Sea Witch so that it blocks the flow of water, and saves your miners—that is, if you have the constitution to keep going?"

"Damn you, Veyron. They're my men. Of course, I'll do it!"

"Good man. Now, I'd be most obliged if you were to avoid getting us stuck, too."

Sam's dive watch made an irritating noise, the kind of grating sound capable of waking the dead. He stared at it, for a moment hoping his vision was playing tricks.

He muttered a soft oath—no such luck.

The timer indicated he was out of Hydrox.

He knew there'd be a few more minutes of residual Hydrox inside his dive helmet, but it was mostly irrelevant now. They had run out of time.

Concealed inside his dive helmet, Sam displayed a broad last smile. The sort he was renowned for, which said, he could have it all.

He and Tom had saved as many as 10,000 people today.

Not a bad way to die.

"Sorry to drag you into this, Tom."

"Not your fault Sam. Had to be done."

The Sea Witch jolted. "Can you see what happened?" Sam asked.

Tom moved towards his nearest porthole. "Well I'll be! Who would've thought, eh?"

"What?" Sam moved toward the porthole and looked out.

"Some idiot just piloted Rescue One into the tunnel!"

Rescue One wasn't trying to turn them around so that they could escape. It was attempting to push them further into the tunnel, so they could block the entire flow of water.

We must be missing something. The water must still be flowing beneath us.

They moved another few feet towards the narrowest point of the tunnel, and then stopped dead still.

Sam's Hydrox supply ran out.

"Some rescue team. They should've come a couple minutes earlier. We've had some fun Tom, but now I'm out. Good luck."

"I have another five minutes. I'll buddy up with you, and we'll get out of here alive."

"The hell you will. We both know it's going to take them a lot more than a couple minutes to rescue you."

"Whatever you like, Sam." Tom moved above Sam and started to attach his secondary rescue regulator to the back of Sam's Hydrox tank.

Sam tried to move away, but he suddenly found his body no longer had the strength to fight it.

The darkness came over him. Not the horrifying obscurity that is taught to us since childhood of death. But instead, a warm, comforting darkness, like a blanket. Something to cuddle up to, and die.

Then there was the intense light.

For a moment, Sam thought the glow might be the radiant light of a powerful oxythermic torch, cutting through the thick hull of the submarine.

But it was followed by more darkness.

And then nothing at all.

※

The thick steel fell away from the submarine. Dumping the oxythermic torch on the ground next to him, Michael peered through the opened hull. Inside, two bodies floated, their eyes lifeless as a corpse.

We were too late . . .

"They're dead," he said to Veyron.

"Bullshit they're dead! Let's get them to the diving bell. It's got a hyperbaric oxygen chamber inside. If they've run out of Hydrox, they've only just run out of it!"

Michael grabbed the first body he could reach and dragged it through the new opening. Veyron took the limp diver and said, "I've got him. You grab the next one, and I'll get him in the hyperbaric chamber."

"Okay."

The diving bell had been relocated directly next to the entrance to the pyramid, and a visiting doctor had remained on board, in case Sam and Tom needed resuscitating.

Michael reached through the moon pool, where the doctor had already removed Tom's helmet. "How's he looking, Doc?"

"His oxygen levels are very low, but he's still breathing on his own," the doctor replied, while holding a 100% oxygen mask over Tom's face and squeezing a bag next to it in rapid, deep, movements to ventilate him. "Quick, get Sam's helmet off so we can start working on him."

Michael and Veyron worked to quickly remove Sam's helmet.

His face was ashen, and it was immediately apparent that he was no longer breathing. Michael slipped a finger beneath the dive suit, and felt for a carotid pulse. "He still has a pulse, but it's weak!"

Veyron already had the bag valve oxygen mask set up. He quickly attached it to Sam's face, and began to ventilate him with 100% oxygen.

"Over here, Doc. Sam needs your help."

Monitoring equipment showed that his oxygen saturation levels were less than 30 % — a reading not ordinarily associated with life. And the heart monitor showed that Sam's heart rate was very slow, no more than twenty beats per minute.

Veyron continued to ventilate him.

"His oxygen levels are coming up, but his heart rate is dwindling."

The doc drew up an injection of adrenaline and then gave it straight into the large vein in Sam's neck.

Thirty seconds later, a stupid, slightly intoxicated kind of grin came across Sam's face.

"Veyron," he whispered in a hoarse voice. "What took you so long?"

※

The next time Sam was awake, he and Tom were inside the dive bell's hyperbaric chamber. His head still hurt, his thinking processes slower. Clearly his brain was recovering from its oxygen starved state.

"You there Tom?"

"I'm here. I knew they couldn't kill you that easily."

"I thought I told you to keep your own damn Hydrox?"

"And since when have I ever listened to your orders?" Tom replied.

Sam tried to sit up, but found himself too dizzy to do so. "Thank you, Tom."

He didn't hear the next words Tom said. Instead he heard the confident, bordering on arrogant, Harvard trained voice of Michael Rodriguez.

"You're awake, Sam. That's great."

"Michael, what are you doing in the dive bell?" Sam slurred.

Veyron approached and stared down at him. "He was saving your ass."

"You saved me?" Sam was confused.

"It turned out that I was the only one left who could pilot the submarine," Michael explained. "It's you and Tom who really saved everyone."

"The miners?"

"They got wet, but they didn't drown—thanks to the two of you. It appears you live up to your reputation, Mr. Reilly."

Sam grinned. "We did it, but there's going to be months of work to seal the other side of the tunnel and bring a team of archeologists down to explore the tomb."

"There is, but you saved them both. Thank you."

"You're welcome."

"I have a proposal for you Sam Reilly," Michael said.

"What do you have in mind?"

"It's something particularly important to me. Much more so than the mine you just saved. I need some time to talk to you . . . but not here."

"Why not here?" Sam asked, stuck inside the hyperbaric chamber, most likely for hours.

"For what I'm interested in, I need to talk to you alone. It's not that I don't trust your crew specifically. I don't trust anyone with what I want to talk to you about."

"Where then?"

"I have a yacht—a traditional Mayan sailboat. We both have work to do to get the next operations underway. You with your archeological dig, and me reestablishing a highly profitable silver mine. Not tomorrow — say the following day, Thursday?"

Sam didn't answer.

"Come sailing with me. Just the two of us. It will be fun, and I can tell you what I need."

Sam had no idea what his most recent billionaire friend wanted, but he was intrigued. Besides, after today's events, he could use a day out sailing an antique sailboat.

CHAPTER 6

The wind was light in the Gulf of Mexico, but the Mayan sailboat even lighter, and as Sam helped to raise its single sail, the little boat picked up speed. Sam grinned, his teeth white as the little ship's sail. He felt like a boy on his favorite theme park ride.

This was real sailing. Between himself and Michael, the two men owned more than most countries spent on their military each year, but now, they'd been reduced to a couple of overgrown children, trying not to fall out of the little boat.

Michael surprised him with his competence. Clearly the man had spent a lot of time on the water. As the midday sun rested above the horizon, the light wind became no wind. Above their heads, the single sail flapped aimlessly.

"Did you bring a little motor?" Sam asked.

"No, did you?" Michael laughed.

"No, I forgot that."

"Do you think the wind will pick up?"

"Not a chance."

"That's okay, that's why I have these." Michael said, showing him a pair of oars. "It's only about three miles back to land. You're in no rush?"

"No," Sam lied.

He watched as Michael comfortably connected the oars to their rollicks and start rowing. Strong chest, back and arms pulled on the oars, the outline of each muscle stood out, well defined. The man, Sam observed, had lost none of his strength over the years.

Sam sat there enjoying the warm Mexican sun and the coolness of its water for half an hour in silence. Michael had brought him here for a reason, and that reason certainly wasn't so that he could forget that the wind stopped like clockwork at midday, so he could have a long row back to the harbor.

He looked at Michael's eyes. They were hardened and focused on the rowing, his jaw clenched, and he was only concentrating on his breathing. Otherwise, his mind could have been a million miles away.

You take your time Michael — it seems I've got all day . . .

After an hour of hard work, Michael finally obliged.

"Let's have some lunch."

"Sounds good," Sam said.

"Have you ever heard of the Mahogany Ship?"

"Which one?"

"Come on, Sam . . . you know the one I'm referring to . . ."

"The Australian legend of the Mahogany Ship?" Sam laughed and regarded the somber expression on Michael's face.

Is this seriously what today's sailing trip was all about? He's interested in an old myth of a shipwreck?

"Of course I have. My mother's Australian — moved to the states with my dad before I was born, but in heart, I still see myself as an Australian."

"Some say it's a myth. Others, like myself, still believe her to be out there, resting somewhere, waiting to be found, with answers for humanity."

"If it ever was there, it's now long gone."

"Is it?" Michael's face was almost curious.

"Yeah, the last reference to it was in 1812, when it was found high up on the sand inland somewhere. Now, ships much older than that have been found to survive in sea water, but not fresh water, and never on dry land. No, if she did exist, and she was out of the water, she's long gone . . ."

"Would you like to bet on that?" Michael's lips twitched into an almost crooked smile.

"I'm not much of a gambling man, but sure. What's the price?"

Michael reached into his pocket, and pulled something out of his pocket. "How about this gold coin I recently found in Australia?"

Sam examined the coin.

It was a golden ducat with the picture of King Charles the V at the front and a Spanish shield at the back. At the bottom of the coin was the date, still clearly marked: 1518.

"The year Ferdinand Magellan left Spain in his attempt to circumnavigate the world," Sam identified.

"Ah, so you know your history? Good man."

"Magellan was a fantastic sailor."

"Yes. Now, did you know that Magellan was born in Portugal, and only came to the King of Spain when his own king had snubbed the voyage? And that the King of Spain, Charles the V, who was eager to challenge the Portuguese dominance of trade routes to India by finding a western route across the Pacific Ocean, offered to fund him?"

"I've read a little about the story. How come?"

"As well as providing him five ships, King Charles V had more than 200 gold ducats minted, specifically for his voyage, in 1518."

Sam didn't bother to hide his now rising interest. "And you think this gold is one of those 200 ducats?"

Michael ignored the question and continued with his history lesson. "This is what we know about the five ships that Magellan was given to achieve his task. The 'San Antonio' was wrecked off the coast of South America, while the 'Santiago' mutinied and returned to Spain. After the death of Magellan in the Philippines, the remaining three ships became too cumbersome for the few sailors who remained. Consequently, the 'Conception,' the largest of the carracks, was abandoned, and the 'Trinidad' and 'Victoria' attempted to return to Spain. The 'Victoria' was captured by Portugal, of course, and the 'Trinidad' became the only one to achieve the circumnavigation and return."

Sam nodded his head, as though he were enjoying the story. "But the 'Conception,' the largest of the five ships, was never seen again."

"Exactly," Michael sounded excited as he spoke. "Lost, without a trace. But I think you and I have an idea about its fate, don't we?"

Sam ran his hand gently over the old coin. "Where, exactly, did you say you found it?"

"It was discovered on a cattle property in central Victoria, Australia, by one of my company's geologists, who was drilling core samples in search of deep alluvial gold."

Sam took the bait, "Okay, you have my attention, Michael.

What would you like from me?"

"I want proof that Spaniards were the first Europeans to discover Australia, which I am convinced they were. I need you to find the final resting place of the Mahogany Ship and her treasure."

Sam smiled. "First of all, if your geologist has truly found this coin deep underground in Australian soil, and you believe it was once from the Mahogany Ship, then surely all your geologist has to do is dig a little. I mean, it's unlikely that the coin and the ship separated that much, if they were both underground."

Sam waited, expecting the man to argue this point. When he didn't, he continued, "As for proving that Spain was the first European country to reach Australia, it's really kind of moot now, isn't it? After all, The Mahogany Ship never returned to Spanish soil and the British took ownership of Australia in 1778 through colonization."

A slight breeze rocked their boat for a moment. Both men raised their heads as if scenting the strength and measure of wind. They smiled and shrugged at the false alarm.

"The British considered Australia *terra nullius* meaning 'nobody's land,' Sam said. "As you can imagine, this didn't please the natives who had been living there for the past 40,000 years. Not that *they* could disagree or have much say. Hard to carry on an argument when you have spears and your opponents have guns." A wry grin came over Sam's lips. "Besides, I'm not a treasure hunter."

"I know that—you think I didn't do some research on you before I came here today? It's precisely because you're not a foolhardy treasure hunter that I want you. After your work on the recovery of the Magdalena, I knew you were the one I needed. The last grand airship now rests at the Smithsonian institute for millions of people to see each year and not locked away in some billionaire's private exhibition, because of you. Besides, this isn't about the treasure. I think I have a fair idea what makes someone like you excited, because, like me, you don't need the treasure. You yearn for something else entirely. You want answers to questions centuries old."

Sam smiled. This rich stranger had worked him out. He didn't care about the treasure, and he sure as shit didn't care which European country wanted to credit themselves with the first discovery of an island that had been occupied by natives, who also had most likely come by boats centuries ago.

"And what questions, exactly, would they be?" Sam asked.

"Could such an engineering marvel as the Mahogany Ship have ever really existed? And if so, who built her?"

"Okay, I'm interested. So, why didn't you just take some big ass bulldozers and dig some more?"

"I already did."

"Oh yeah, what did you find?"

"An intricate system of underground caves, primarily filled with water."

"And you believe the coin came from one of those caves?"

"Sure do. Would you like to go exploring?"

"Are you aware the Australian Shipwreck Act prevents looting?"

"I am, but this isn't about the treasure. It's about answers. How did such an exquisite ship ever end its seafaring days in the middle of a desert? Who built it? And how in the world did such a monstrosity sail using only wood?"

"Okay, partner," Sam said, mimicking Michael's friendly tone. "You can count me in. When do you want to start?"

"Let me know what you need and I'll have it flown with you

on board my jet, tomorrow."

"Okay, but I'll have to leave the Director of Operations in charge of the cleanup here, including the archeological exploration."

"Do what you have to, but join me tomorrow."

"Done," Sam replied, never one to be indecisive. He shook his head, knowing he'd been railroaded, yet he smiled good-naturedly when he agreed.

"That's great," Michael said and flicked a switch behind his seat. A small motor kicked into life, and the Mayan boat started to cruise towards the beach. He gave Sam a slightly sheepish laugh before saying, "I had it put in, years ago, when I discovered the capricious nature of our winds here."

Sam joined him with his laugh, and wondered fleetingly whether he had just joined partnership with the devil.

Sam caught Tom in the galley, eating his way through a family-sized pizza. The smell of pepperoni filled the air as he explained that he had somewhere else to be right now. Tom couldn't believe his friend would abandon him at the point of such an amazing archaeological discovery.

"You want to leave me to conduct the most important project of our career, while you go off looking for a shipwreck that you already think is probably a myth?" Tom's threw his pizza slice down in disgust, while his voice betrayed his incredulity. "This is your project—you're the only one who's even heard of the Master Builders."

"Calm down. I won't be gone long," Sam said, picking up the last slice. "Two weeks, max. In that time your recovery and exploration of the pyramid will still be in its infancy. I'm barely allowing you to lay down the groundwork."

"Something's not right, Sam. I don't buy this story." The slightest of creases formed between his brows, displaying a concern he rarely visibly displayed.

"Don't you want to run the show?" Sam asked, shrugging off Tom's concern and taking a bite of a hot and fresh pizza. Sam shut his eyes for a moment, savoring the taste.

"You know I don't have a problem with that. It's the other thing that I'm not happy about . . ."

"What?"

"Sam. You and I have been best friends since I became the first person to ever beat the hell out of you at the 400-meter swimming meet in junior high school." He frowned with disgust. "Then your dad let you skip school, so you could train every day until you beat me at the finals, bastard."

Sam laughed, in recollection of good times.

"We have very few secrets between us, Sam. Heck, I even gave you the heads up that I was about to call off my engagement to Sarah. The only secret you've ever kept from me is what the hell happened in Afghanistan. Now, on the discovery of a ruin, which you tell me has something to do with an ancient race of Master Builders, and that has to do with the secret that you discovered in Afghanistan, you're not even going to wait and run the archeological dive? Just so you can have a look at some old ship, which, if legend is correct, was never carrying anything of value and was left to dilapidate. Besides, it most likely had its timbers cut for firewood. No way. I don't believe it . . ."

"It is precisely because of that secret, that I have to go . . ." Sam replied mysteriously. "I'll return in two weeks, at the most. Soon, you'll understand."

"If the Mahogany Ship was so important to you, why don't we both go after it, when we complete this job? Then you can put the full force of Deep Sea Expeditions behind the search."

"The Mahogany Ship was the first shipwreck hunt I ever went on with my father and Danny. We got close, too. There were a number of legitimate leads, but after two months, the three of us had to concede that it didn't exist. But I always knew it was out there, and there's no way I'm going to let some rich kid, who inherited the earth—or at least half the valuable ores held beneath it, to literally stumble upon it by chance. No, this is my find. I want to make certain it's done right!"

Tom could see Sam was emphatic. "Okay, and what about you?"

"What about me?" Sam asked.

"How are you going to dive on your own? Who are you going to use for your support crew?"

"Rodriguez is going to dive it himself, and there's an Australian commercial diver on his team, as well as a geologist. Also, Rodriguez has a team of riggers who will provide topside support."

"Do you even remember how much trouble you got into the last time I left you alone on a treasure hunt? I mean, you nearly died without my help, searching for that missing airship, the Magdalena."

"The Magdalena was loaded with treasures of immense value."

"And, you think the Mahogany Ship wasn't?

"It may have been once, but by the time the first westerners arrived in Australia and laid their eyes upon it, the treasures were long gone, or else stolen."

Tom pushed back from the table. Not a scrap of pizza remained. "What about the Spanish coin?"

"There may be a treasure chest worth of Spanish gold coins,

but that sort of money isn't anything worth interesting a man like Rodriguez about. I mean this guy has personal worth in excess of 25 billion U.S. dollars. He has no family, making him unencumbered, as well as one of the richest individuals on the planet."

Tom wasn't convinced. "In my meagre experience of treasure hunting, things that stay missing have a way of making people go crazy with desire and lust. Have you considered why such a billionaire is even interested in the damn ship?"

"He already told me. It's a matter of national pride. He wants to prove that one of Magellan's ships was the first to find Australia."

A concerned frown marred Tom's face.

"Don't worry about me, I'll be fine."

"Okay, but I'm going to need an archeologist to get a better idea of what we've found," Tom said.

"I agree, and I've already contacted just the right one."

"Really? Who?"

"Bill — one of the best archeologists alive. I've wanted Bill on board with Deep Sea Expeditions ever since my dad suggested the program years ago. I've already made the call . . . Bill will be here in the morning."

"William? What's his last name?"

"No, it's just Bill."

Tom racked his mind to recall where he'd heard that name before, but he didn't think he had. Somehow, Sam had never mentioned a man named Bill.

Michael Rodriguez smiled as he examined the list of requirements for his special project. It was long, detailed, and expensive. None of which mattered to him. Sam had asked him for the day to think about what would be required, and if he could leave his crew to help manage their current project.

Precisely two hours after being returned to the Maria Helena, he had written back with his demands. He wondered how Sam had procured such an extensive list in such a short time.

Yes, I've found just the right person to serve my needs, Michael mused.

CHAPTER 7

The massive, purpose built cargo jet landed at Sydney International Airport with a rough jolt. It was technically an Airbus A380, but despite the original airframe, it resembled a supersized military cargo jet, crossed with the extravagant luxuries more often associated with a Columbian drug lord.

Sam's eyes caught the sun from outside the window, and he turned his head to avoid it.

"Is it nice to be home, Mr. Reilly?" Rodriguez asked.

"Home? No, I was born stateside. This is my mother's country . . . but it does feel like home, sometimes," Sam replied. "Now that we're here, are you going to tell me where you discovered that Spanish coin?"

"In some hills, west of a country town called Bendigo. Customs will clear us shortly, and then we will be on our way."

Fifteen minutes later the ship was back in the air.

"You bribed customs?" Sam mused.

The Spaniard smirked. "No, of course not, but men of means have their ways."

An hour later, the A380 landed on the small dirt runway,

near Bendigo. It was a feat Rodriguez had told him cost him millions in engineering modifications to reduce the landing and takeoff distance for the monstrous aircraft to less than an average Airbus.

Even so, the massive aircraft used up every inch of the tiny runway, whose owners could have never predicted that such a mammoth plane would ever have need of it.

The engines, thrown into reverse to assist in braking, threw giant plumes of dirt up into the air, before the expert pilots turned her at the end of the runway. The aircraft then made its way along an open field to the side of the runway and made its final stop. It would sit in the open for the next few weeks.

Sam casually strolled down the plane's automatic stairs.

A rusty sign read *'Welcome to Bendigo.'*

At the rear of the aircraft, the giant loading ramp below the high-mounted tail was retracted. More than ten tons of dive equipment, cables, and drills were already being loaded onto the five Mercedes-Benz G63 AMG SUV six-wheel drives. Each vehicle was then driven off the aircraft.

Sam walked toward the cars.

This was the sort of flamboyant finesse that his father would put on such a vehicle. He had requested a robust four-wheel drive SUV for use on this trip, given the location of the drill site. But only Rodriguez and his own father would have purchased five million-dollar plus luxury SUVs, which looked more like military hardware.

Still, he couldn't help but admire their raw beauty.

"Do you like them?" Rodriguez asked.

"Certainly. What's not to like? It's a sports car, built for a battlefield."

"And the Australian bush is a battlefield. Come, let me take you for a drive."

Sam sat in the driver's seat of the massive SUV. The steering wheel was on the left hand side, having been built for Americans, but that wouldn't cause any problem where they were headed. The front windscreen was raw in its vertical beauty, and not only bulletproof, but it was Pilkington blast resistant glass.

Rodriguez directed Sam out of the town, towards the east. After ten minutes the blacktop road turned to dirt. Another ten minutes later and any semblance of road disappeared completely, only to be replaced by the rugged bushland of his mother's land.

Sam put his foot down and the brutal 5.5 liter, bi-turbo V8 roared into life.

The bush was dry, and large eucalyptus trees spotted the otherwise barren horizon. After an hour's drive, Rodriguez pointed toward a hill in the distance.

"It's up there?" Sam asked.

"I know what you're thinking. The cave system is obviously below the height of the mountain, but that's where we found the Spanish ducat."

Sam looked around at the barren mountain in the distance. "Strange place for the Mahogany Ship to finally rest."

He then drove up the hill.

A large tent had been set up to house the exploratory equipment. It looked out of place in the dry, barren land.

A single man emerged from the tent and watched them, his hands in his pockets.

Sam parked the big truck, waited a moment for the red dust to settle, then he and Michael got out.

"G'day. My name's Frank Edwards," the man said, striding

up to Sam with his hand outstretched. The stranger was noticeably shorter than average, with thick arms, and a large beard concealing his face. It gave him the appearance of one of Tolkien's Dwarven miners.

"Pleased to be working with you," Frank said, gripping Sam's hand firmly. "I read about your exploits with the lost airship, the Magdalena."

Sam Reilly stared down the dark hole in the ground.

It looked unnatural in the otherwise rugged Australian bushland. Just slightly wider than his shoulders, it was far too deep for Sam's gaze to reach its black ending. The entrance had been reinforced with concrete and steel. Below every foot, a reinforced iron ring supported the earthworks behind, forming a natural ladder. It looked professionally built, as he would have expected from the mining operation that built it.

Frank gulped a drink from his water bottle, and then offered it to Sam. "After our first core sample returned the Spanish coin, we decided to drill a larger one so that we could reach the cave system below. You can imagine how excited we were. Particularly after I had contacted Mr. Rodriguez and he'd brought up the mystery of the Mahogany Ship. We really half expected to breach the opening and find the ship intact."

Sam stepped back from the hatch, unable to see any further. "And once you reached it?"

"Then we found a cavern made out of limestone, which appears to form the entrance of a maze of underground water systems, so enormous that . . ." Frank stopped, failing to find the right description and then said, "You'll just have to see it for yourself, mate. I can brief you better once we get down there."

"Okay, so how deep is this thing?" Sam asked.

"Five hundred feet, but the cavern opens nearly 50 feet earlier."

"And at the bottom of the cavern, is it dry?"

"No, the entire cavern is flooded, approximately halfway up, but there's plenty of evidence that the height of the water has risen and fallen many times before."

"How can you tell?"

"Byron, our geologist, noted that the rock formations on the walls have hundreds of lines within them, spreading from the very submerged ground, through to the surface high above the water line. Most likely indicating the changing erosion of limestone via the flowing river," Rodriguez explained.

"So, it's safe to say that the Spanish coin didn't sink through 450 feet of soil to reach the cavern. Therefore, it must have entered at a point further upstream, where the difference between the surface and the underground waterway is smaller." Sam said out loud, speaking to no one in particular. "And if that cavern is a hundred feet high, then it's conceivable that the Mahogany Ship, if that is indeed where the Spanish coin once originated, may be further upstream."

"Let's go have a look then, shall we?" Frank said, as he pressed the green button hanging from a cable that dangled inside the mineshaft, "After you, Sam. It's only big enough for one person at a time. Byron's already down there. He will look after you once you're at the bottom."

Sam peered over the side again and spotted it.

The miner's elevator—a makeshift, cable driven device, used to gain vertical access down the narrow shaft. It was a ten-minute journey to where a team of miners had already constructed a large work platform, from which to base their expeditions.

Sam stepped onto the steel platform of the miner's elevator as it reached the surface, "I'll see you at the bottom, shortly, shall I?"

"I'll start loading some of the equipment you brought and meet you down there soon," Rodriguez said. "Frank will follow and bring you up to speed with where the underground operation is progressing."

The dry heat of the Australian outback disappeared along with all external light as Sam began the long descent. After several minutes, the shaft opened up to a massive cavern, and a large grin came across Sam's face at what he saw.

Four large spotlights had been bolted into the walls and were projecting light around the room, allowing the enormity of the cavern to be fully visualized. Not quite as large as the one that held the Magdalena for 75 years, the cavern commanded a similar interest over his imagination. Below, the water lapped around the newly constructed work platform, which was approximately 50 feet in length by 20 feet wide. At the southern end, a small computer station had been set up, and three laptops displayed geophysical information.

These people aren't amateurs . . . but why then do they need my help?

The water was flowing, but without any tremendous strength. It would be easy enough to dive. There were five tunnels through which water fed into the cavern and only one out of which it drained. Taking a cursory glance at it, Sam could see that only two tunnels were large enough for a ship to travel, but that didn't mean that the ship wasn't stuck further up one of the smaller tunnels. On the platform a man prepared dive equipment.

Sam pressed the red button on the lift controller and it came to an abrupt halt, approximately half a foot from the work platform, causing him to nearly slip.

"Welcome to the Mahogany Cavern. My name is Byron."

"Mahogany Cavern?"

"It's just what Mr. Rodriguez named it when the coin was found here."

"He's quite convinced, isn't he?" Sam eyed the man in front of him. He was clean shaven, with thick glasses.

"That we're going to find the Mahogany Ship? Yes. He says he had a hunch when we first found the coin, and then metallurgy analysis placed it around the same time that Magellan's ship would have been in this vicinity." Frank shrugged his shoulders. "In my experience, Mr. Rodriguez's hunches are always right. If it came anywhere near here, we'll find it."

"Time will tell whether or not it was a myth or something much more interesting, after all," Sam replied, with an indifference that he didn't feel. "So, there are five entrances and one exit?"

"No, actually, there are five entrances and two exits . . . one of them is far below the water line . . . come around to the computer station and I'll bring you up to speed with what we have discovered so far. We've had three men down here including Mr. Rodriguez, who has told me he wants to be involved every step of the way. You've already met Frank—he's our drilling engineer. And then there's me. Senior geologist for Rodriguez Mining Inc. You now make the fourth person who even knows of its existence."

"You guys look pretty set up here. All of you must be used to working in similar environments. Why doesn't Mr. Rodriguez bring in a full scale team and mine this ship? Why me?"

"It's a good question. I'm surprised Mr. Rodriguez didn't talk to you about it before you came. The land that we drove

95

through to reach this shaft is private property. It's farming land — cattle to be precise. We haven't purchased the license to mine here, because with the exception of the gold coin, our exploratory core samples show no gold deposits. As far as the government's concerned, this is still an exploratory expedition. You, my friend, are the fourth person who even knows of the existence of that Spanish coin."

"Couldn't he get a grant to dig specifically for the Mahogany Ship? I know that the Victorian government, seeking to find the answer to the mystery, offered $200,000 to anyone who could locate the remains of the ship. I'm certain they would offer exploration rights for that purpose."

"Yes, but it would take months, if not years, to get around the bureaucracy. Outsiders would come in and take over. Besides, it's going to become complex. You see, the land above us is on the corner of three separate properties. Depending on which tunnel our mysterious ship lies in, we're going to have some difficult negotiations. But if we can continue as an exploratory team, for which we already own the rights, and then come across the Mahogany Ship in all its remaining glory, then . . ."

"You're merely a mining corporation that is now helping bring a name to the local community."

"Right, you've got it. So, you see, we can't just go around blasting our way through these tunnels, pumping out the million plus gallons of water in the process. We need an expert cave diver, with experience in treasure hunting."

"I wouldn't call myself a treasure hunter, but I've been involved in a few expeditions to find lost wrecks over the years. I would be lying if I said I wasn't interested in finding the Mahogany Ship, so here's to hoping that your boss's luck hasn't run out just yet." Sam smiled. "All right, now down to work. Let's see what you have explored so far."

Byron slid his hand across his laptop screen four times, revealing a new system, "This is a geological scan of the cavern and tunnels that we've reached so far. Using ground penetrating radar, the computer has been able to predict size and shapes of the tunnels. The red arrows show the direction of water flow."

Sam looked at the screen, which displayed a map that looked more like an ant's nest than a cave. There were five tunnels in and two out. Two of the tunnels looked quite detailed, with the map going nearly a mile down each of them. The rest of the tunnels stopped for no apparent reason within a hundred feet.

"You've explored the first two tunnels, is that right?"

"Yeah, we can set the SONAR up at the entrance of each new tunnel, but it only works based on line of sight, so we need to physically move it further up the tunnel to capture each new section."

"And the other three tunnels?"

"Five tunnels, you mean?"

"No, three tunnels. At this stage, we're working on the theory that the gold must have come from further up the tunnel, which is where we will find the Mahogany Ship, if it was ever here."

"Okay, each of them are going to be a bit more trouble. You see, there, the tunnels open into more tunnels, which then open into yet more tunnels. To complicate things more, the tunnel depths change dramatically, both raising and dropping more than a hundred feet. At some sections, it's wide like this cavern, but in others, it begins narrow enough that you and I might only just reach our way through it. In other words, it's going to be a cave diver's nightmare."

"No, this is the type of challenge we dream about, but it's

going to take some time." It had already become clear to Sam that it could take years for a team of divers to explore this underwater labyrinth.

"Time that we don't have," Rodriguez said, as he came down the mine elevator.

"No, I understand that. So, we're going to have to narrow our field of search a little."

"And how do we do that?"

"Okay, I've laid eyes on her . . . now let's get the rest of my equipment down here, and I'll show you just how we're going to solve this mystery."

CHAPTER 8

The Sea King helicopter dropped the new team of arrivals on the deck of the Maria Helena. Keeping its rotors turning as the passengers disembarked, the pilot took off again, as though the precious minutes it took to fully allow its rotors to cease spinning was too much. They were the latest of a set of arrivals who'd come to assist in their work uncovering the underground pyramid and its mysteries. It was the third inflight the past 24 hours, and the Maria Helena was starting to fill up, mostly with scientists, engineers and microbiologists.

Tom Bower shook his head.

It had never ceased to amaze him how much a man like Sam Reilly could obtain when he thought it was important. Even if, in this case, he was making certain that Michael Rodriguez was going to foot the bill for every piece of equipment that had arrived. But it wasn't equipment that surprised him. It was the professionals who came. Each one the top of their respective field, they had been brutally poached from whatever expedition or project they had formally been working on and whisked from any location on earth to help.

To do so required money and power. Both of which, Sam's family had in abundance.

He looked at the flight manifest. Ignoring the other three

passengers, whose roles would most likely be limited to that of lab technicians aboard to examine artifacts and sea life, Tom's eyes reached the name of the man he wanted to meet.

Dr. Bill Swan.

The four passengers stepped out of the helicopter and moved towards the main cabin with military efficiency. Each one carried an identical large duffle bag over his shoulder. They could have all been top of their field scientists — nerds — but they meant business.

Tom took notice of the only woman amongst the new arrivals, as the only one who didn't appear to be a scientist. Her features were clearly part Southeast Asian, but her height betrayed her European heritage. She was wearing olive cargo pants and a light tank top. Her face displayed all the signs of a person who hadn't slept much in the past 24 hours. There were slight bags under her almond shaped hazel eyes and her messy dark hair had been tied back in a careless ponytail, a pair of Ray Bans propped on top.

Matthew shook her hand as he greeted them all at the rear of the Maria Helena, and despite her obvious fatigue, she responded with a warm smile, full of perfect white teeth. She could have been a model.

I bet that smile's gotten her whatever she wanted many times before . . .

Tom wondered what such a beautiful woman was doing aboard their ship. Already, he'd decided to make it his mission to find out. He would have approached her directly, but first he needed to meet the new archeologist Sam had sent him. Work would have to take priority over pleasure.

Tom approached Matthew after the group of new arrivals were shown to their respective living quarters, "Have you seen this person?" Tom pointed to the name Bill Swan, "This man."

"Bill, the archeologist?"

"Yeah, that's the one."

"Sure have..." Matthew laughed.

"What's so funny?"

"Did Sam tell you that Bill was the best archeologist he's ever met?"

"Sure did. In fact, he told me specifically, that he has asked him to join Global's Deep Sea Expeditions since old man Reilly first put him up to running the project, but each time was rejected. This was the first one that grabbed Bill's attention enough to bring him out. Why, do you know him?"

"Yeah, I've never met Bill. But I've heard the rumors." Matthew's left eyebrow was raised, as though he was trying to hint at something, "Sam's been trying to get Bill to join his team for nearly a decade. Rumor has it they studied together at college, but I've heard that it was more personal than just that. Either way, I don't know how he's managed to persuade Bill to join us..." Matthew then laughed again, "Only it's not Bill... its Billie. She often uses the name Bill on her dissertations, because in our apparently equal world, people still take more notice of a man's view."

"Holy shit! You mean that angel who came in just then is the archeologist that I have to look after for the next two weeks until Sam gets back?"

"That's the one, you lucky bastard."

It was at that point that the angel returned.

"Matthew, I just spoke to Veyron..." she said, her waspish voice betraying her adorable face in a second. "That fucking asshole sends a couple of his goons to pick me up and virtually drag me from a research core sampling station, 20 miles deep, in Antarctica, a week before my two-year project reached its conclusion, starts telling me a whole bunch of bullshit about finding one of the greatest archeological discoveries of this century—and now I find out he's not even here. I don't even know how he found me..."

Matthew just smiled at her as she stopped her rant.

"How did he find me?" she asked. "Has that fuckwit been keeping secret tabs on me again? You know that's why I left him last time. I was sick of the secret bullshit that seemed to follow him wherever his projects led. So, Matthew, tell me . . . where the fuck is he, and what's more important to him than this amazing discovery?"

"The Mahogany Ship," Tom replied, not making an attempt to conceal the grin that beamed across his face.

"Who the hell are you?"

"I suppose I'm the man who's going to be your tour guide of the deep blue sea over the next couple weeks until Sam returns."

"Billie, meet Tom Bower. Sam's Director of Operations and the Maria Helena's helicopter pilot. He's been friends with Sam since they were kids," Matthew said.

"You're Tom Bower?" She looked him up and down with what appeared almost like admiration. "I kind of expected you to be bigger. Sam spoke a lot about you while we were at college. You both became helicopter pilots for the Corps . . . only he got out and you stayed and served your country at the Sandpit . . ."

That's strange. He neglected to mention anything about attending college with a half-Asian goddess with a foul mouth . . .

Instead of mentioning it, Tom replied, "Yeah that would be me. You two must have been pretty close. You sound like you know him pretty well."

A crooked smile appeared, but even that looked delicious.

"Yeah, you could sure say that again."

There was obviously a past between the two of them, but she certainly wasn't going to be forthcoming about it.

Matthew, on the other hand, held no such restraint, "Sam and Billie have a past that goes way back . . . Are you kidding me, you haven't heard the story?"

"No . . ." Tom started to reply, but was interrupted.

"And he's not going to either," Billie said. "So, he's finally discovered the Mahogany Ship, hey?"

"Sounds like it," Tom replied.

"Okay, I have to actually run this ship, so I'll leave you two to get better acquainted," Matthew said.

"Thanks, Matthew," she said. "So, why aren't you there?"

"What do you mean? I'm looking after his real work."

"I thought you two were like best buds or something."

"So what?"

"So, Sam Reilly's been after the Mahogany Ship since he was a boy, searching for it with his dad! No wonder he left this project in an instant. He's been obsessed with it ever since I met him. What I don't understand is why he wanted to go after it alone?"

"Yeah, well that makes two of us." His recent feeling of betrayal echoing in his voice, Tom said, "It sounds like the Mahogany Ship's already been discovered and he just had to go there to make certain it was over, and didn't want to lose what we've discovered here."

"All right, so what have we discovered here?"

Tom looked around, determining which of the newcomers

were within earshot of their conversation. He trusted the crew of the Maria Helena, but who could say where the loyalties of the specialists who just arrived might lay?

He walked to the back of the boat, where their conversation was less likely to be heard by anyone else aboard. "How much did Sam tell you about it?"

"Not much."

"Really?" He didn't believe her. "You left your project of two years, and flew half way across the planet, to join a man I'm not even convinced you like, at a new project, which you know nothing about?"

"Like I said, a couple of his goons literally dragged me off my research station in the Antarctic. All Sam told me on the phone was that he found what appears to be a very old Mayan Tomb in the shape of a pyramid, at the bottom of the ocean. Don't get me wrong, that sounds pretty interesting, but nothing that couldn't wait until next winter, after the hurricane season. He certainly didn't suggest that he'd discovered Atlantis or something like that!"

"Did he tell you how big it was?"

"No."

"Well its big . . . you just need to look at it for yourself. Anything I say about it won't do it justice. It appears a local mine damaged part of it while blasting deep below the pyramid, releasing a thousand-year-old cyanide store, which set into motion the destruction of most the sea life within the Gulf of Mexico."

"How did you get around that?"

"We've filled the section with concrete. A team of mining engineers are now installing a more substantial plug on the other side of their mine's tunnel. We're now excavating our side of the pyramid again. There's more to go, but there will be enough for you and me to enter the pyramid."

"Anything else that might shed some sort of explanation for why Sam was so insistent on bringing me in on this case? Anything that can help before we dive tomorrow?"

"Yeah, do the words Master Builders mean anything to you?"

Billie's face didn't change at all, as she replied, "No, never heard the words before. Certainly not in the Mayan culture." It was so casual, that Tom's experience working as a SEAL kicked in — *did she already have an answer to that question prepared?*

"Not at another site or project you and Sam worked on previously, perhaps?"

"Not any that I can recall, but I know that Sam's worked with a number of archeologists over the years for a variety of projects. I'm sorry, Tom. It was nice to meet you. I'll see you first thing in the morning, say 5 a.m.? I have to check on something."

"Yeah, 5 a.m. I'll see you at the moon pool. Welcome aboard, Billie. Let me know if I can do anything for you."

She nodded her head and left quickly.

At 0500 sharp, the diving bell began its slow journey to the bottom of the ocean. Neither spoke as it descended, and Tom noticed that the slightest appearance of concern had not left her face since he'd first mentioned the words Master Builders.

"You said that you studied with Sam?" Tom asked.

"That's right. Why do you ask?"

"You studied archeology . . . what else did you major in?"

"Ancient maritime archeology."

"You were looking for Atlantis?"

She laughed, "No, I'm searching for something very different, and much more elusive." Billie said, mysteriously. "Not that I don't believe Atlantis existed. That's for certain, but the shape of the world would have been very different all those years ago. It was probably some other land-based civilization that became buried with the turn of an ice age."

"Then what drew you towards the ocean?"

"It's a long story."

"Was that how you met Sam?" he pestered.

"No, that's a different story." Her smile told him that there was a lot more to it than that, but that she wasn't going to reveal her and Sam's history. "Let's just say, I'm a third generation archeologist, and I'm still trying to find the answer to a question which plagued my grandfather his entire life."

"What was he looking for?"

"Materiana — A mythical lost city in the clouds."

"I've never heard of it," Tom acknowledged.

"The search for its answers drove my grandfather insane — or so we thought, until it got him killed. Obviously, someone took interest in his research."

"Did your father continue with his research?"

"No, my father knew better. There are people out there who would kill to find it, and those who would kill to keep it a secret."

"And that's what you were searching for in Antarctica?"

She looked out the porthole and replied, "No, that's just what drove me to the field of maritime archeology. Like my father, I know when something is too dangerous."

Her evasive answer only served to intrigue him more, but

he could see that he was making her uncomfortable.

"Was it Sam who introduced the Master Builders into your world?"

She ignored the question and continued reading the known schematics for the mine below the pyramid from her tablet.

There was no way Billie was going to be pushed into speaking about the Master Builders—even though they were now deep under water, where prying ears would struggle to listen.

As the dive bell reached the bottom, the two geared up and prepared to commence their dive.

"Are you ready for this?"

"Let's see it . . ."

The tower looked grand up ahead.

"It's not as large as Sam made out. It looks similar to the great pyramid of Giza, but nowhere near large enough."

"Just wait until you see what lies beneath the sand. Veyron has left a dive hub on the seafloor, in front of the pyramid's entrance. A place where we can base ourselves over the next few days while we work."

Slowly, they kicked their fins toward the entrance, and then descended the tunnel. At the very end of the tunnel, his flashlight shined on the remains of the wrecked Sea Witch.

"Yours?" she asked.

"That one was Sam's idea. He used it to stop the flooding of the mine below us. A desperate attempt, and one that nearly got us killed—but it saved a lot of lives."

"That sounds like my Sam."

To the very left of it, a small hole had been drilled, just big enough for the two to swim through. On the other side, the tunnel narrowed and descended vertically. At the very bottom, Tom turned down the tunnel to the left.

"What's that way?" she asked.

"About a million tons of concrete. That's the side that had the leak. It's been filled with concrete, and the owner of the mine is paying for it to be repaired and then excavated from the other side."

"Gotcha..."

They dived the next hundred feet down the diagonal tunnel, which ran along the inside of the pyramid.

The pressures were tremendous and the tunnel narrow, playing havoc on the most seasoned diver's emotions. Many, without any previous knowledge of claustrophobia, would discover a fate worse than death in such a place.

"How you doing?" Tom asked.

"I'm fine... I've been in much worse places than this," she teased. "How about you?"

An image of the incident that nearly killed him last time he was inside the pyramid's tunnel flashed across his mind. It was no more than a second, but enough to give him pause before he spoke.

"I'm fine... just so long as the walls don't cave in on me this time."

He shined his bright flashlight down the tunnel. Its powerful LED light shined like a laser, reaching the bottom of the pyramid.

"There it is... the bottom."

"I can see it."

Making the sharp turn, and with self-regulating neutral buoyancy built into their dive suits, it was disorientating whether or not they were now moving laterally, diagonally or vertically. Tom, a confident cave diver, felt the reassurance of bubbles floating on the top of the granite blocks above their heads, allowing him to orient himself.

They were now level.

A little over a hundred slow kicks with his fins and the opening to the first of the three chambers came into view.

It still glowed.

"It's glowing?" Billie voiced her surprise.

"Yeah, it sure is."

"Do we know what's causing that incandescent light?"

"Some sort of large crystal at the center of the King's Chamber that radiates straight through each level of the tomb."

"Somehow drawing light from above?" she suggested.

He kicked his flippers gently, propelling himself closer to the entrance ladder, and replied, "No, that's what we assumed at first, too. Then, when we stayed overnight, the light seemed to just keep glowing."

"Any ideas what would make that happen?"

"None. We were hoping you might just find out for us, because we sure don't have any idea."

"Must be some sort of marine creature . . . or element that radiates light . . ."

"No, it's not that simple . . .

"What do you mean?" Billie's voice betrayed her surprise, "Why not?"

Sam gripped the first rung of the ladder before replying, "You'll just have to see it. Can you make it up that ladder?"

"Sure can," she replied, climbing with the additional 80

pounds of dive equipment as though it were nothing. She was fit, that was for sure.

Tom followed her and, climbing into the first of the three chambers, removed his dive helmet.

Billie paused, "Are we certain it's safe?"

"The cyanide?"

"I'm an archeologist, but even I know how lethal it can be."

"It's safe, but just in case, our life support watches will let us know if there are any changes."

"And the air in this room?"

"It's good. We should have several days' worth of oxygen to look after us."

Tom left all of the equipment they would need for the next few days at the first chamber, and they climbed the ladders to the second and then up and into the last one. The King's Chamber.

Watching her enter the room, Tom saw her reaction immediately . . .

"Motherfucker! He's found the Master Builders . . ."

CHAPTER 9

Sam gripped the throttle of his dive scooter, propelling himself towards the dark tunnel ahead. Two had already been searched thoroughly, but this was the first opportunity that he'd had to travel through any of them.

The tunnel was wide, providing ample room to maneuver the specialized underwater craft. With its narrow lines, it resembled a miniature torpedo more than the life sustaining dive machine that it was. Its propellers broke hydrogen bonds that formed to create water, releasing oxygen for the rider. In addition to its carbon fiber dive tank, it had the ability to provide enough breathable gas for its rider, up to 5 hours.

He wasn't going to need anywhere near that length of time today. Instead, Sam planned a simple half an hour trip to see how far he could get. He'd already seen the sonar images of the tunnels—now he wanted to see it with his own eyes. Searching for the Mahogany Ship, which had managed to remain hidden for so many years, required something more along the lines of as well as science.

Once the timer on his scooter read 30 minutes, he dutifully brought it to a stop and examined his surroundings. The landscape of the tunnel had change little throughout the time. It was a combination of more than a hundred limestone caves, joined together and eaten away from eons of erosion by the water through the soft rock.

This one was no different.

Around him, he noted that the tunnel, although reasonably wide, would never have permitted a ship as enormous as the Mahogany Ship to travel down its path. He thought about it for a minute or two, and then took a sample from the limestone silt, placing it in a tube marked 'Tunnel Three.' If a ship had ever passed through this place, he was going to find some evidence of it through a detailed analysis of the microscopic particles found inside that tube.

Finding a shipwreck is an art, but that's no reason to ignore science . . .

Over the next few hours Sam proceeded to make the same investigations of each of the five tunnels. The water was cold, but it wasn't freezing. His dry suit had an inbuilt heating device, which had maintained his core body temperature at a comfortable 98 degrees Fahrenheit.

When he returned to the dive platform, Michael and Frank were already waiting for him.

"You all right Sam?" Frank asked, helping take some of the heavy weight of his dive equipment off him as he climbed the ladder.

"I'm fine. Why do you ask?"

"You were down there longer than I was expecting."

"I was just getting a feel for these caverns. You'd be surprised by how much you can learn by watching the flow of water through tunnels such as these. The old gold miners who panned for gold used to understand the river systems better than we do today. A good gold prospector would watch the river for days and days before digging his spade into a single chip of soil. By doing so, he could ascertain where the heavier, gold filled, sumps might be."

"And what did these rivers tell you?" Frank sounded interested.

"I don't know yet. I've taken core samples where any man-made products might become lodged. Still, it's been hundreds of years since the Mahogany Ship disappeared, so who knows what could possibly remain? As for the river system herself?" Sam's intense, steel blue eyes, stared at the man, before he said, "Despite two of the five tunnels being large enough for her to come down, there's only one in which she could actually have made it down without tearing herself apart on the rapids."

"So then we only have to explore the largest of the tunnels?"

"No, the reality is, it could be somewhere upstream of all five of the tunnels. Just because the coin made it down doesn't mean that the Mahogany Ship ever made it this far. Your boss isn't going to be impressed, but there's a very high probability that, if the ship ever entered this river system, she's resting hundreds of miles further upstream."

"Which means . . ."

"It might take months, if not years, to explore all of the tunnels."

"Okay, let's get the gear," Billie said. A wry smile over her beautiful face told him that she wasn't going to talk about them.

Tom decided that he'd had enough of the cloak and dagger story. He was running this show. Whatever involvement the Master Builders may have in this, he had a right to know. He said, gently touching her shoulder to stop her, "Who were they?"

"I don't know what you're talking about."

"No more lies, Billie. Sam brought you here for a very specific reason, didn't he? And I have an idea it had something to do with the Master Builders."

She shrugged her shoulders.

"Tell me. Or you can go back to whatever it was you were doing in Antarctica before Sam dragged you out here."

Billie looked like she was seriously considering abandoning the site. Then she turned to face him. Her almond-shaped brown eyes stared at his and then conceded. "These markings here," she whispered. "They were made by them. Only, there's never been any evidence that they ever made it across the Atlantic, until now . . ."

"But who were they?"

"They were builders — engineers to be exact, and very good ones. Think of the ancient wonders of the world."

"I'm not an archeologist, but I thought the Egyptians built the Pyramids?"

"That's what we thought until recently, but since then new evidence has shown that a superior race, known as the Master Builders, built them all . . ."

"So why wasn't the information published?"

"That, my friend, is an interesting question. I'm sure your friend Sam Reilly is probably one of the few people on this planet who know the real answer."

"Afghanistan, 2003?" Tom knew exactly what she was referring too, but didn't know why.

"Come on . . . you never believed for an instant that your friend was honorably discharged after three weeks in the Sandpit?"

"No, and he never told me what happened, so I didn't ask."

She sighed. "Yeah, well he broke a code, and opened the doors to an otherwise unreachable research path. And the existence of the Master Builders came to the attention of the National Security Agency."

"The NSA?" Tom looked confused. "What would they care about some ancient civilization?"

"Okay Tom, have you been to Egypt and stood at the base of the Pyramid of Giza?"

"Yeah, many years ago. Sam and I went there on our summer break."

"Do you honestly think a four-thousand-year old civilization could have built something like that using technologies that predated the invention of the wheel?"

"Yeah, yeah, I've heard all the stories before. It's an amazing feat, but somehow they managed it. I read a theory once about using really big whips or something."

"It doesn't matter. Have you ever wondered if we could build the same structure using modern technologies?" Billie asked.

"The thought's never entered my mind. Why?"

"The answer is, we're still not capable of it. Each of those blocks weighs as much as 15 tons. To place one at the top of the 481-foot pyramid would be impossible. Each block is so perfectly positioned that not even a hair could be slid through it."

"Okay, so how did they do it?"

"They didn't."

"Who did then?"

"The Master Builders."

"What, like aliens?" Tom laughed, and then noticing she was serious, said, "Okay, so how did they do it?"

"No one knows, but if a civilization that lived more than 4000 years ago had technologies superior to ours today, we want to know about it. And if their knowledge is still out there, then the U.S. military perceives that as a threat."

"And that's what Sam got himself involved in?"

"Yes," she whispered, as though someone could somehow be listening to them at this depth, inside a granite vault. "Only, they were watching him. He never told me what he was involved in, specifically. He brought me the information he needed analyzed and that was it. But I knew he was being watched. Eventually, he couldn't take it anymore, and that was when he returned to the ocean, and to working for his dad."

"Or did he get a lead he knew was going to get him killed?"

"Like what?" She asked.

"Maybe he discovered something and knew his only hope would be to find it when others weren't looking?"

"Only Sam can answer that question."

Tom focused and then said, "So, where did these Master Builders go? What killed them off?"

"We have no idea. In fact, there have been theories to suggest that they never died, but there has been no evidence."

"An entire civilization more advanced than we are lived 4000 years ago and there's no proof that they existed or died out? Seems pretty farfetched to me."

"Not an entire civilization . . . only a handful of people."

"What do you mean? I thought these people built the pyramids?"

"They were the engineers. They were hired by the kings and

rulers of the day to build grand things and then instructed thousands of slaves to perform the tasks. Slaves who, without their guidance, could never have built anything so mighty."

"So what was the most recent build of the Master Builders?"

"The Pyramid of Giza—nearly 4000 years ago. Until now. Sam tells me this pyramid appears to be less than 1000 years old. Now, unless there was some kind of cataclysmic oceanic event that no one has even heard of in the past 1000 years, which has submerged this pyramid, I would say the ability to build more than 200 feet underwater a perfectly-shaped pyramid, so exacting as to entrap air inside its three chambers so that 1000 years later we are able to breath unaided here, makes this place pretty much impossible."

"If Sam knew they were here, why did he involve you, or anyone for that matter? Why not fill the entire place with concrete, cocooning it for another 1000 years?"

"Because, like me, he needs to find the answers."

"But, if he's so obsessed with secrecy, why not stay here himself?"

"I've no idea why he's chasing the Mahogany Ship, but he brought me in on the secret, and knows that I won't betray him." Billie took a photo of the ancient text on the wall above her.

"What is it?"

"It's an old text, written in a very old language."

Tom looked around the room.

It appeared to be cram packed with pictographs and hieroglyphics. He hadn't even considered whether it was a language. "Egyptian?"

"Sort of—to anyone other than an expert in the Egyptian language, it would appear to be just that."

"But?"

"Most of this room is filled with Mayan texts, but not this one here. This one stands out as something entirely different. It's much older than Egyptian, more difficult to understand, and only ever used by the Master Builders."

"How many people know this language, if it even exists?"

"I'm not sure. There's myself, Sam, and an unidentified man from the NSA. We think Russia and France may have their own team working on it. Even we don't fully grasp the meaning of all of it. But, I'm pretty certain Sam and I are ahead in the race to crack it fully."

"What does it say?"

"I don't know precisely. It's just words. Nothing that makes sense. I'll have to put it into my laptop to get a better translation."

"And it's definitely created by the Master Builders?"

"Sam thinks so. We don't even know for certain the Master Builders were real. In some Egyptian texts, they are referred to as the Ancient Ones."

"All right. Why don't you finish taking these pictures and I'll go retrieve the laptops. Then, maybe we can get to the bottom of this damn thing."

"Sounds good, thanks."

Tom spent the next half an hour carrying her laptop and equipment up to the King's Chamber. Walking into it, he noticed her tall, lithe figure standing on top of the sarcophagus. She was in her element. And she looked happy. He stood there quietly for a minute or so, and then realized he could have watched her all day.

She was beautiful, intelligent, and one of the most single-mindedly focused people he'd ever met. And she had by far the foulest language of any person holding a doctorate. The thought made him laugh.

"What the fuck are you laughing at?" she asked, leaning a little further outward.

"The fact that, for a leading expert in an ancient language, you have the worst use of explicit English words."

Above, Tom could hear her chuckle at his comment without taking her attention off what she was doing. As she leaned further out, the back of her loose fitting shirt lifted up, revealing a slim back and a tattoo of a pyramid on top of a mountain.

He couldn't help but feel that it made her look sexy, while at the same intriguing his imagination. *Where did that pyramid come from?* He wanted to ask her, but there were too many other questions on his mind, and besides, he didn't want to draw attention to the fact that he'd been staring.

She took another couple of pictures and then turned to climb down again.

Tom's eyes, distracted by her tattoo and the top of her black sexy underwear, now noticed, tucked into the back of her pants, a Glock.

Why the hell would she be carrying that?

Billie then jumped down and switched on her laptop. Her camera was automatically synchronized with her computer.

She ran the data.

"What do you think?" Tom asked, careful not to mention that he'd just noticed she was carrying a weapon.

"I'm not sure yet. It's currently running a decoding program," she said. Tapping a number of keys in quick succession, Billie turned and said, "Okay — that proves it. They're definitely a match. This chamber was built by the

Master Builders."

"That's great. Do you have any idea what those words say?"

She pressed enter, and the screen started to flick through the images, comparing it to all previous known texts by the Master Builders, before stopping. "Got it."

"What did it say?"

She turned the laptop so he could see it.

Ajtzak waits for his lost twin in the final revelation.

"What the hell does that mean?"

"Ajtzak was the name of the king who's buried here," Billie mused, "By the sounds of things, he was a twin. But he lost his brother before he died? I don't know how, where, or why."

"That's great, so he lost his twin brother, but that doesn't bring us any closer to understanding who they were, where they achieved their knowledge and most importantly, why they disappeared."

"No, but the fact it was written in the ancient language shows that this man was a Master Builder, and so was his twin brother. Wherever the hell he is." She looked up at the walls, and then said, "I'm just hoping to find those answer somewhere within these walls before the NSA removes them."

"What do you mean, removes them?"

"Every time we find a clue to the puzzle, they destroy it."

"Then we'd better make sure we get the answer quick this time," Tom said, still wondering how he was going to get her handgun.

CHAPTER 10

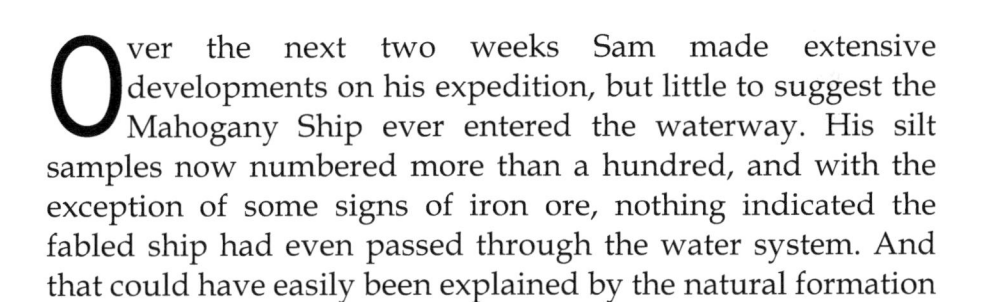

Over the next two weeks Sam made extensive developments on his expedition, but little to suggest the Mahogany Ship ever entered the waterway. His silt samples now numbered more than a hundred, and with the exception of some signs of iron ore, nothing indicated the fabled ship had even passed through the water system. And that could have easily been explained by the natural formation of iron oxide within the natural rocks further upstream.

Sam and Frank split the tunnels into three separate sections, dividing them so that each person could cover more ground. Each of them would explore two small tunnels for a distance of two miles or until the tunnel became too difficult to dive. Afterwards, both of them would dive the fifth and largest of the five tunnels. Michael Rodriguez had left to attend to company business for a few days. He had made it clear that if any discoveries were made, they were to wait for him, because he wanted to be there when the Mahogany Ship finally revealed herself. Byron, the only one who appeared positively out of place below ground, remained at the Mahogany Cavern to maintain communications, and make projections based on the data being brought in.

None of the four smaller tunnels returned anything

substantial. Not so much as a nail was found. It was time to search the final tunnel and live with the results, whatever they may be.

On the fifteenth day, Sam discovered something that sparkled.

Nearly a mile upstream in the largest of the five tunnels, he spotted it. His flashlight carefully filtering the area from right to left, it was so faint, for a moment he thought his mind was playing a trick on him.

The he saw it again.

Just the tip was sticking out of the sand. Sam swam towards it, his pulse quickening.

His hand reached in and pulled it from the sand. When he turned it over in the water, the sand disappeared, revealing the head of the king of Spain, Charles V.

Behind his facemask, his grin returned. *It was here. The Mahogany Ship must be somewhere nearby!* Sam turned to the metal detector again. If the water flowed in such a way as to capture the heavy gold coin in its sediment at this exact location, there was a good chance there would be more.

Instantly, two more sources pinged.

Following the increasing pings, he found two more Spanish coins. He inspected each carefully. All three were identical to which Rodriguez had initially introduced him. Sam was ecstatic with his find. He would finally prove the existence of the Mahogany Ship. At the back of his mind, he was surprised by the condition of the coins—the water made them look like they had just been minted.

He dismissed the thought and pocketed all three of the gold coins.

Securing one surreptitiously in a double zipped pocket,

which would beat any scrutiny if required, Sam felt guilty at the thought of stealing from Rodriguez. But he needed to be certain, and this was the only way he could think of doing so.

Sam marked the spot on the sonar map, and then said, "Frank, we have a hit."

He could hear the excitement in Frank's voice. "That's great! What have you got, Sam?"

"A gold coin! Two of them, actually."

"That's great news. Stay where you are, and I'll return to your location. I'm a few hundred feet ahead of you."

"Copy that."

Sam and Frank used up the remainder of their air supplies searching the area, with no other discoveries that day. When Sam finally climbed out of the water and onto the work station in the Mahogany Cave, he was met by Byron, who'd already brought out three bottles of bubbly.

"Congratulations," Byron said, handing him a full glass of champagne.

"Thank you. There's our proof that the ship once entered this water system. Now it's only a matter of time before we find the Mahogany Ship," Sam said taking the glass. "Does Michael know, yet?"

"Yes, I've contacted him. He's in Spain, but says that he will be back in a few days. He also wanted me to remind you not to enter the Mahogany Ship before he returns."

"I still have to find it first, but you can reassure him that I won't enter it without him."

Frank climbed the ladder behind him. "I think we just did it Sam. We now know that she sailed somewhere upstream of that tunnel. Now, all we have to do is follow it."

"Like I said to Byron, now that we know where to look, it's

a matter of when we find it, no longer if," Sam replied, shaking Frank's solid hand.

"Do you want to come into town to celebrate? I know a great pub that does fantastic food and locally brewed beer," Frank said.

"Sure, sounds good. I have to contact my skipper and see how my project's going in the Gulf of Mexico, but I'll come into town after that."

Taking one of Rodriguez's Mercedes six-wheel drives, Sam drove into town.

He found a small post office at the end of Main Street, and walked in.

"Hello," he said to the little old lady who operated the store, which appeared to rent movies and act as a general store as well.

"Hi dear. May I help you?"

Sam pulled out a novelty birthday card. At its center was the image of a sun and a slogan saying 'Happy birthday, I hope this brings you plenty of luck and sunshine for your special day.' He smiled deceitfully, and said, "It's my daughter's birthday tomorrow. Any chance, I can send her this card, to this address by then?"

She looked at the address, and said, "Portland, Oregon? That's a long way from here. I suppose you're with those mining fellows?" Sam nodded his head, as if to acknowledge her intuition was correct, causing her to smile. "It will be close, but as luck would have it, this week's postal flight is due to take off in another hour. You might just be in luck."

"Thank you," Sam said, as he started to write in the card.

Dear Elise,

Happy Second Birthday, I hope it's a great one, and I'll see you in a few weeks. He followed the note with a number of XX and OOs. Tell mummy I'd like to know what treasures you found for your birthday. She can contact me through the normal system.

He then sealed it in an express post and handed it to the lady.

If only they knew they were handling a 2 million dollar coin.

The next morning, Sam entered the tunnel feeling pumped. Greeting Frank, he said, "You ready to find this ship today?" Somehow, he could sense the Mahogany Ship was getting near.

Over the course of the next four days, the two men searched more than 15 miles of the tunnel, with no sign of the ship. No sign of more Spanish coins, or parts of the ship.

By the end of the week, Sam walked into the tent in which Frank and Byron were eating breakfast and said, "It's not here."

"What have you lost?" Frank replied casually.

"Not just lost, not here."

"Come again?"

"The Mahogany Ship, she's not down there," Sam said.

"Not down there?" Frank cut another large piece of meat off the steak, and continued eating as he said, "Then where'd the Spanish coins come from?"

"I've no idea, but a ship that large would have displaced something visible by now. If the coins were brought there by a ship, then some other remnants of that ship must be too."

"So, you're done then?" Frank stuffed another bite of meat into his mouth.

"Not done yet. Just haven't worked out our next move and far less convinced that the Mahogany Ship was ever here." Sam leaned up against the Mercedes six-wheeler. "Can Rodriguez get me access to a helicopter?"

Frank stopped chewing for a moment, then replied, "Yeah, but it will take a few days. He can bring it in on his A380 when he arrives in another three days. Will that do?"

"No, I don't want to wait that long. I noticed a little Robinson 22 parked at the airport. Any chance we could borrow her?"

"I'm sure you could hire it. It's probably used for cattle mustering. I'm not sure about a pilot though."

"That's fine, I can fly it."

"Okay, where do you want to go?"

"I need to clear my head," Sam said. "But more importantly, we've run out of ideas inside this tunnel. Now I want to see the land from above. Get an idea of where the Mahogany Ship might have once been. Those coins didn't get there by magic. Something's taken them there, which means that a real river must feed into these tunnels."

"And you want to find that river?"

"That's the plan."

Byron stood up, looked at his phone and then started to talk to someone. Five minutes later, he returned to the conversation. "Brent Higgins is the owner of that helicopter. As expected, he owns nearly 20,000 head of cattle around these parts, and uses her to muster them. I've just hired it on your behalf for the rest of the month. If you head that way after breakfast, he said he'll have one of his mechanics fill her up."

"Thanks Byron. I think I'll skip breakfast and wander over there now."

"Suit yourself, and be sure you take care on that machine.

Mr. Rodriguez told me under no uncertain terms that I'm to ensure your safety. He believes you alone can lead him to the Mahogany Ship."

Sam laughed at that and then replied, "We're still yet to see if he's right."

By ten a.m., Sam had traded his trusty Mercedes for a Robinson 22, and was in the air. It provided a unique view of the landscape, and he hoped that the solution to his problem would present itself when it was ready. He spent nearly six hours flying and refueled three times before he found what he was after — a river more than forty miles upstream, which fed into an underground cave. The entrance was by far too small for a ship to enter, but that didn't mean that two hundred years ago it wasn't large enough to fit the Mahogany Ship.

Sam landed next to it.

Looking at the steadily moving water, he threw more than a hundred plastic floating devices, no larger than a marble, into the river below. Each contained a small camera, transmitter, and were electronically numbered to match the name of the river. He continued this process until he reached another four rivers.

Back at the Mahogany Cavern, a wireless receiver waited for the information. It might take days, but he would have his answers.

Sam reached the entrance to the mine shaft by the early afternoon, landing right next to their sleeping tents. He switched off the mains, letting the rotary blades settle, and then stepped out of the helicopter.

Frank walked towards him, and asked, "How did you go?"

"Good," Sam said as he grinned like the owner of a winning hand at cards. "And, I'm pretty certain I know where we're going to find the Mahogany Ship."

"What's taking so long, Frank?" The pitch of his voice betrayed Rodriguez's impatience. "This was supposed to be over two weeks ago — we have a timeline to keep!"

"There's a lot of tunnels to explore, it's going to take time, sir."

"Yes, but couldn't you give him a hint?"

"And risk him catching on? No way — he's a bright man. He could ruin this whole thing if we try and rush him." Frank coughed. Years of smoking left him with a perpetual chest infection. "He thinks he knows where she is."

"Really, and is he right?"

"Yes, but it beats the hell out of me how he came up with it, after spending the day in the air, sightseeing in a helicopter."

"Did he now? That's interesting. Keep me informed."

"I will Mr. Rodriguez."

CHAPTER 11

Billie looked at the collection of images on her second laptop, unable to find exactly what she was after, swiped the screen to the left and began her search again. By the eighth one of these, she heard Tom's annoyingly cheerful voice.

"You seemed pissed off about something," he said.

"No, just unable to find what I'm looking for. For the most part, this tomb is precisely how I'd imagine it. But then, when I look closely, I discovered that something's wrong."

"Like the presence of the Master Builders?"

"Yes, but it's more than that," Billie said, enlarging an image of the room, taken from the floor. "Look at the picture. What do you see?"

Tom laughed, "I'm a helicopter pilot by trade, and an expert cave diver, but art was never one of my specialties."

"That's fine. All the more this will make sense to you. So, what do you see?"

"I see a turtle floating in an ocean, surrounded by thousands of stars, and a giant tree strangling the entire universe."

It was Billie's turn to laugh. "All right, an interesting interpretation. I see what you mean about art not being your strong point. All the same, you spotted what basically appears to be a number of Mayan depictions."

"Really. Were they on drugs at the time?"

"No. The Mayan people pictured a universe consisting of heavens above and underworlds below, with the human world sandwiched between." Billie enlarged a simplified diagram of the Mayan world. "The heavens consisted of 13 layers, stacked above the earth, and the earth resting on the back of a turtle, floating in the ocean. Four brothers called the Bacabs, possibly the sons of Itzamná, supported the heavens. Below the earth lay a realm called Xibalba, an underworld in nine layers. Linking the three realms was a giant tree whose roots reached into the underworld and branches stretched to heaven. The gods and the souls of the dead traveled between worlds along this tree."

"And the king was at the top of the 13 layers of the heavens?"

"No, this room depicts the king at the bottom, having just left the lowest rung of the earth based ladder."

"You look like you know a lot about this stuff."

"I've read a little. I'm no expert on the Mayan belief system, but for the most part, this seems to be in keeping with Sam's original theory that this was a Mayan tomb. There's just one thing I don't understand."

"What's that?"

"There's a lot of references to non-Mayan symbolism."

"Could they have been drawn from the Master Builders?" Tom suggested.

"It's unlikely. If the Master Builders did exist, they have never mixed more than one culture in their projects. The only image that carried across from the African relics, Egyptian pyramids, and other ancient sites is that of the Master Builders themselves. In this case, it almost appears as though the Mayans, themselves, have collected the information."

"Could the Mayans have traveled that far?"

"Around the world?" Billie drew back from her monitor, and paused for a millisecond. "Anything's possible, but highly unlikely. Such a statement would be akin to saying that the Vikings were the first to sail around the world."

"So what are you going to do?"

"I need to get some more pictures. Actually, I'm going to need hundreds of them. If I can feed them into my computer system, I have a deciphering program that may be able to come up with an explanation."

"Do you have any ideas?" Tom asked.

"Yes, but none of them are possible."

"Why not?"

"Because it suggests that the Mayan people once had something more powerful than we have today."

"And what's that?"

Billie grimaced, like she was about to say something ridiculous. "The ability to actually travel between their realms of life, death, and the heavens. Some of these images show cultures that weren't even developed a thousand years ago."

"That is crazy."

"Yes, it is. I just don't have a more plausible answer—yet."

In front of her, Billie's computer hummed as it tried to crunch some very complex algorithms. Despite being one of the most advanced laptop computers in existence, it was having trouble resolving the data that she had input. Billie had taken more than three hundred pictures of the pictographs and hieroglyphics inside the King's Chamber. Having charted the information on her laptop, she now tried to decipher what it all meant.

And this meant differentiating between the Mayan texts, Egyptian symbols and Master Builder markings.

She had remained at the original site, gathering as much information as she could, before word of its discovery reached them. Billie knew what would occur when that happened, and if she was going to get any further in her search, she would have to have it all mapped out before they came.

A pinging sound could be heard coming from her computer.

That was quick.

Billie sat down and looked at her computer screen. Its advanced program, designed specifically to develop answers about the theoretical race known as the Master Builders, had discovered something about the room, but what, she had no idea.

Do you wish to read the report now? Y/N?

She clicked yes, and instantly several pictures of the roof of the chamber began filling the screen. The emphasis of each image appeared to be the blue glowing light at the center. It resonated from a ball, small enough to fit in the palm of your hand, but capable of resonating enough light to allow them to see throughout the entire pyramid. The same unexplained light source radiated down from the inside of what must have been the pyramid's capstone, and then passed the missing scepter on the king's sarcophagus, and then through the narrow shaft that extended eight levels below, to the bottom of the pyramid.

Yes, I already know there's no logical explanation for the light.

Billie flicked through the slideshow. Slowly at first, and then faster, before she spotted it. Something was changing in each slide, but it wasn't until she had clicked through more than a dozen that she realized what it was.

Holy fuck — somebody's been watching us.

At the center was the source of the blue light, and where the perfectly round, blue crystal sparkled like a diamond, stood a shadow. The shadow formed and then moved throughout a number of slides, as though someone—or some*thing*—had been watching them.

"Tom, we've got trouble." She shouted the words without thinking about who was listening.

Tom walked across the room, his camera still in his hand, and replied, "What have you found?"

"Just look at these pictures."

She watched him flick through four or five images, and then stop. Pointing at one of the little shadows over the stone of light, he asked, "Does that look like something inside keeps moving?"

"Yes. Someone's been watching us while we work!"

Opening the black bag strewn on the floor next to the laptop, Tom withdrew a chisel and hammer. Climbing on top of the enormous sarcophagus, he said, "Whoever they are, their camera's going to be destroyed in a second."

"Wait!" Billie said.

"What?"

"Is that wise? I mean, won't they know that we know they've been watching us?"

"Maybe. Or maybe they'll just see that the lens has been

destroyed. Either way, I'd rather them not follow what we're doing here."

"What if they come for us?" she asked in no more than a whisper.

"Come for us? We're nearly 300 feet deep. We have our own dive team manning the diving pod at the entrance of the pyramid. They're going to notice if someone comes down here."

"Sure, but what if they're already here?"

"No way. Did you see any secret hiding places? I mean, we've just spent the last two weeks studying this place. It's all granite. The only way in here is from below the pyramid, the way we came. If someone comes, we're going to have the upper hand."

She nodded her head and then said, "You're right — get rid of it."

Tom examined the round blue ball, which, now that he really looked at it, appeared similar to the lens of a camera. Without studying it further, he took the hammer and chisel, and struck the corner hard.

Nothing happened.

Tom studied the object again, before striking it with the hammer alone. Nothing, not even a crack. "I've got no idea what they made this thing out of, but it's strong as a rock."

"Try the masonry behind it. Whoever put it there, probably used a protective cover," Billie suggested.

He struck it again, but even the masonry seemed firm.

By the fifth attempt, Tom stepped down.

"Here, try this. It's a diamond tipped chisel. Should slice straight through whatever that is."

"Thanks," Tom said, as he picked it up, angled it right at the crystal ball, and struck it with the hammer.

Again, nothing happened.

Tom placed his eye right up to the lens of the crystal. Not even a scratch could be found. Staring at it, despite the light that the ball was emitting, he noticed that it appeared dark inside, giving him the slightest doubt that it even was a camera lens.

"Come on up here. See if you can get a better look at this thing, will you?"

Billie laughed. "Sure. You want me to show you how to break it?"

"I'm not sure you're going to want to, once you've examined it. I mean, the thing looks pretty old. I don't see it being a camera so much as a looking glass."

Below him, Billie, started to climb up the sarcophagus. "Whatever it is, there are few materials in existence that can withstand the tip of that chisel."

Tom stared at the glass again, and then said, "Whoa!" nearly falling backwards off the sarcophagus. "What did you just touch?"

"Nothing. Why?"

"It wasn't nothing. And it just changed the view inside the ball!"

"What the fuck do you mean, changed the view inside the ball?" Billie said, her nostrils flaring as she tried and failed to climb up to see it.

"I mean, someone's been watching this place, all right — and for a very long time!"

CHAPTER 12

Billie's fingers, unable to reach the top of the enormous sarcophagus, slipped as she tried to climb up its sharp walls.

Tom shuffled down, and asked, "Want a lift?"

"Yeah," she replied, wishing she didn't need his help.

"Not a problem," Tom said, lifting her onto his shoulders.

His hand, she noticed, slipped, catching her butt for support—remaining there a moment longer than it should have. And then he quickly removed it before she said anything. Billie reached further, and caught the top of the stone block, allowing her to climb up.

For a second, she wondered if Tom had meant to place his hand there. The minor indiscretion was soon lost in her desire to see the looking glass.

She stepped up onto her tippy toes, so that she could place her eye right up to the optical lens. On the other side, Billie could see a room. It was similar to the one that she was already in, and at its center, another sarcophagus—only this one didn't appear Mayan at all.

Forgetting about Tom's actions, she said, "Do you think that whoever's been watching us is in the room directly above us?"

"No, I think they're farther away than that," Tom replied.

"Farther away? What are you talking about? Now that I'm up here, I can see that this thing is only a few inches long, and clearly shows the room above."

"That's not possible. I've already done the basic arithmetic, and a few feet above us is the entrance to the pyramid. There's no way there's another room. Besides, didn't you notice that wherever that looking glass seems to end up, it too, looks down upon a room, not up?"

"You're right," she said, chiding herself for letting her nerves affect her usual circumspection. "Before, when I was climbing, you said that I did something to change the image here, is that right?"

"Yes, I don't know what you did, but whatever it was, the ball went from a dark, impenetrable blue, to this clear, window into what appears to me to be another tomb."

"That's what I was thinking. Okay, help me down, I'm going to retrace my steps and see if I can change it again."

"You're the boss," he said, without wiping the grin off his face.

Ordinarily, she would have sworn at him for his behavior, but she was too enamored with their discovery to even think about him. He had an attractive face, and was mostly harmless.

She climbed down and then up the base of the sarcophagus a number of times. "Any changes?"

"Nothing," he replied.

"There must have been something," she said, and then saw it. Along the base of the cradle for the missing scepter, stood a small wheel, with a number of jagged edges, giving it the appearance of the cog on a bicycle. She counted the edges.

There were thirteen in total. She gave it the slightest of turns, and the largest of the twelve stone spikes now pointed in another direction. "Anything?"

"Yes, what the hell did you do?"

"Not much. I just rotated this stone dial. Why, what do you see?"

"It appears to be a giant cave. There are markings on the walls, but nothing that means anything to me."

"Interesting," she said, turning the dial again, "and now?"

"Another tomb."

"The first one we saw?"

"No, this one seems smaller. And the markings are different."

Suddenly, she no longer saw the wall of the sarcophagus as a number of indiscriminate pictographs, from seemingly random places and cultures throughout history. Now, it appeared as though it were a map, with the power to see different parts of the world.

She quickly examined the other images on the wall. There was a petroglyph of the Congo River, the pyramid of Giza, and a Siberian rune with an inscription.

Rotating the stone again, she asked, "What do you see?"

"Another room. Only this one is definitely bigger. It appears to be the final resting chamber of three separate kings."

Her eyes then spotted a pair of Atlantean rings and bar.

She turned the dial again so that the stone spike and the image perfectly aligned. "What about now?"

"You're not going to believe this," Tom said.

"Try me."

"It appears to be the remains of a ruined city . . . and the city is submerged. The water is clear, and appears shallow, the sunlight from above sprinkling through, as though from the ripples of the waves on the surface. There are structures in the distance and they're covered in–"

"An orange metallic material," Billie finished the sentence for him.

"Yeah, how'd you guess?"

"Because I just pointed the dial towards Atlantis."

Billie took a step back and then ran at the sarcophagus. With two nimble paces, she was standing on top of it and said, "I have to see it!"

"See what?" Tom asked.

"Atlantis!" she screamed.

"I thought you weren't interested in Atlantis?"

"No, I said that I wasn't searching for it, which is very different than not wanting to see it when it literally appears before you."

She moved closer towards Tom, trying to get as close to the looking glass as possible. On the tips of her toes, her hand gripped his for balance. She felt his other arm instinctively wrap behind her.

Closing her left eye so that she could focus on the looking glass, she saw the little blue light. At first it was opaque, but then her eyes began to make sense of the turbid vision on the other side.

A ruined city appeared.

It was submerged by water, and appeared close to the

surface, as though it had remained hidden all these years in no more than thirty or forty feet. Glimmerings of light from the ripples of the ocean above could still be seen. And on the walls of the remaining structures, an orange metal.

"My God — it is Atlantis!" Billie said, and then, kissed him on his lips.

"What was that?" he replied, an attractive smile, bordering on absent confusion, radiating fondly.

She was still holding on to him and noticeably let go before explaining, "See this orange material?"

"Yes . . . it looks kind of like bronze and copper."

"Only it's not. It's Orichalcum!"

"What the hell's that?"

"Orichalcum is a kind of fabled metal, described in a number of very old writings, most notably, the Critias Dialogue recorded by Plato. Orichalcum was considered second only to gold in value, and only ever found and mined in Atlantis. A vibrant orange in color, it was thought to be an alloy, containing a unique combination of gold, copper, zinc, iron and lead, with gold the highest percentage."

She saw the pupils in Tom's beautiful hazel eyes swell.

Few, she noticed, were immune to the allure of Atlantis. "If it was an alloy, can't people simply mimic it?"

"No. What made Orichalcum so unique was that it wasn't a manmade alloy, at all. Instead, it was a naturally occurring ore, which was mined. Despite knowing the mix, the alloy can't seem to be reproduced, artificially. One theory is that volcanic activity molded the combination of raw materials into the unique alloy. This, in turn, has led many archeologists to search for Atlantis where ancient volcanoes are now submerged. But there has never been any real proof that it or Atlantis even existed — until now."

Tom stared at her perfect face.

It was only for a couple seconds, but maybe, just too long. Billie, he decided, had the rare combination of an almost demure smile, perfect teeth, and brown captivating eyes. Right now, those eyes sparkled with excitement, making her even more attractive, if that were possible.

How such a face could harbor an intelligent mind yet explode with such offensive language simply baffled him. Nonetheless, he would have paid a very high price to kiss those lips again.

"Do you understand what this means?" Billie asked, stepping back. Tom reluctantly let go of her firm back.

"Hmm . . . That you'll forgive Sam for dragging you away from Antarctica?"

"Yes. Wait, no. I'm still pissed as all hell about that. This means we just discovered something that's been lost for more than two thousand years!"

Tom noted that she made no reference to the kiss. It was an accident, brought on by her excitement, and nothing more. Trying to focus on their discovery instead, he said, "There's just one problem."

"What's that?"

"We still have no idea where that looking glass has been taking us."

She stopped looking, and looked back at him. "You're right. But there must be some way to find out. I mean, it isn't electronic. It's just some form of translucent crystal. Atlantis must be close."

"Are you sure?"

For the first time since he met her, Billie looked uncomfortable, as though there were a crack in her certainty. "Yes, of course. Why?"

"Because you told me that the map below showed images from Siberia through to Africa. Which means, apart from now seeing the image of that ruined city, we're no closer to discovering it than the rest of the world in the past two thousand years."

"That's where you're wrong," she said.

"How so?"

"Because we know that it's real."

The two spent the rest of the day exploring the thirteen ancient visions through the looking glass. Billie thought she must understand what Alice felt like when fell down the rabbit hole. Her entire world had changed in the space of a few hours. She had just about given up finding any more leads on the Master Builders, and was ready to return to the surface, when the discovery of the looking glass occurred.

It wasn't until well past midnight that she finally went to bed. Unable to sleep, her mind kept returning to the events of the day.

The discovery would change everything.

She had hoped it would be there too, but despite looking throughout the entire map, there was no evidence of what she'd really been looking for.

The Lost City in the Clouds

Billie had been looking for it since she was just six years old. Ever since her grandfather first introduced her to the myth, but like him, she knew that it was real. One day she'd find it, but this tomb wasn't going to provide that answer.

She put the thoughts out of her mind. So much had happened, and there was so much more that needed to be done.

And there was the kiss, too.

That, she thought, was a surprise. It was an accident, of course—she'd never mix business and pleasure. But it was unexpectedly nice, too.

In the sleeping bag a few feet away, Tom, despite lying down only minutes before, appeared to be sound asleep.

Figures . . .

She watched him for a while. She'd never seen someone sleep so soundly. She recalled his face after she'd kissed him. He almost looked hurt that she hadn't mentioned anything about it afterwards, and then, like a gentleman, he carried on with the pretense that nothing had happened.

And nothing would happen . . .

It had been a long time since she'd been with a man. She'd accepted long ago that the hunt for the *Lost City in the Clouds* had taken its toll on her social life. But that was expected for any woman trying to achieve something in the male dominated world of archeology.

She closed her eyes, and imagined herself kissing his boyish lips.

It was unexpectedly pleasant . . .

It would be nice to accidentally do it again . . .

What made the matter worse was her knowledge that she was the one who held the power in the relationship. Tom had already given away his hand—he wanted her, that was plain as day, in his pained face. *The pained face that I caused him . . .* But she did have the ability to change that. She could have anything she wanted.

And why shouldn't I?

When she couldn't find an answer to that question, Billie slid out of her sleeping bag. Being naturally warm blooded, she slept in nothing more than her underwear. Next to her were her cargo shorts, white shirt, and handgun. Her first instinct was to get dressed, but the sight of her weapon stopped her. She still hadn't told him about it. Carefully, she concealed the weapon with her shirt, leaving all three on the ground, and walked towards Tom.

"You awake Tom?"

He made no response.

She stood up, and approached him, still uncertain what she wanted. It wasn't until she saw his innocent, sleeping, face that she decided what she really wanted.

A girlish grin crossed her face as she realized what it was.

"That Motherfucker!" she swore loudly, forgetting what she was about to do.

Tom sat up instantly, looking as though he was ready to kill any intruder. "What?"

"Up there on the wall!"

He jumped up, grabbing the hammer next to him as a though it were a deadly weapon — and in his, it probably would be.

"I don't see anything. What is it?" he whispered.

"It's right there . . . the Mahogany Ship!"

CHAPTER 13

At the entrance to the mine shaft, Sam looked at Frank's serious face and said, "What if we were wrong about the coin having to come from further upstream?"

"No, that can't be right. The coin didn't travel on its own. The river would have been required to move it to where you found it. Therefore, the coin must have entered the river upstream, and then flowed over the centuries until it became imbedded in the soft, limestone sediment."

"You're right about the coin having come from further upstream, but what if the Mahogany ship continued sailing downstream, taking with it whatever treasures she was carrying?"

"Shit, you're right!" Frank replied. "Why didn't we think of that? Of course, the water level has been changing heights over the centuries. If the Mahogany ship somehow entered the water system, it's conceivable that it then sailed silently further downstream, until it reached a point where its size precluded it from further movement."

"It's hard to imagine a ship of that size moving through a cave system at all, but the tunnel would be large enough."

"Would it?" Frank asked.

"I'm sure it would."

Frank opened the computer documents containing known measurements of each of the tunnels. Pointing to the only exit tunnel, he said, "No, it's only forty feet high. There's no way anything as large as what the Mahogany Ship was described as could possibly get through there."

"Unless its masts were destroyed?"

"Even then, would the thought of a forty-foot ship sound like the description that the survivors of the Emily Rose gave of the Mahogany Ship?"

"No, but would you trust the description of a bunch of starving survivors to provide an accurate account of the ship?"

Raising his left eyebrow, Frank countered, "I would have been surprised if they all gave the same inaccurate one."

Sam paused his speech for just over a moment. He knew he had the right answer, but just didn't quite know how to prove it.

His eyes then lit up.

"No, I know what happened. It's so obvious—I can't believe we didn't think of it earlier. Come on, we have work to do."

An hour later, Sam and Frank were standing at the diving platform inside the Mahogany Cavern. Their equipment checked and then rechecked, they were about to put Sam's theory to the test.

Opening his dive tank to full, Sam said, "A similar thing happened with the Magdalena—a lost airship from World War II, filled with Jewish treasure. The silt had built up over the years until she was sitting high and dry."

"But the tunnel's still below the waterline," Frank replied.

"Yes, but I realized what the movement of silt could do in 75 years, then in the 200 years since the Mahogany Ship was last seen above ground, the size of that tunnel could have changed extensively."

"You seem pretty certain of yourself."

"I've spent a lot of time trying to make sense of all of this. It's the only explanation."

Sam then placed the mask over his face, and pin dived into the water below. The two Seadoos were tied up, just below the work platform. He waited for Frank to follow and start the little electric motor on the Seadoo, and then took off in the direction of the flowing water.

It only took a couple minutes to reach the entrance to the downstream tunnel. For the first time since he arrived, Sam noticed that it appeared to form an incomplete semicircle, imagining just how large it could be if that circle had been allowed to be completed.

He drove his Seadoo to the base of the tunnel's entrance. The sand was deep. It would take weeks to dig it out to know for sure, but it certainly looked like the depth of the tunnel could be doubled if the sand were removed.

"How far have you traveled down this tunnel?" Sam asked.

"We haven't. We all thought that the Mahogany Ship could have never gotten this far."

"All right, here's to hoping that she lies on the other end of this tunnel."

Sam then drove his machine into the tunnel, his powerful LED headlight shining on the long passage ahead. The flow of the water was stronger, having been fed by the other five upstream channels. He was glad that he was using his motorized Seadoo and doubted very much that he could swim against the current if he had to. In the back of his mind, something told him that he should have run a safety line, but he was too eager to know the truth.

Nearly an hour later, Frank drove towards him, "Sam, how much further do you want to go?"

"Until we reach the Mahogany Ship," Sam replied.

"Are you sure? We haven't set up for a prolonged dive."

"Yes."

Sam continued, at full speed.

Frank asked, "Don't you want to stop and search the areas that we've already covered?"

"No. If it's here, we'll see her."

Sam looked down at the energy marker on his Seadoo. It was reading orange. He had plenty of power left. A little more than half what he started the day with, but the return trip, against the current, was going to exhaust a lot more power.

He continued, driven on by the mad desire to find the fabled ship.

Frank tapped on his dashboard and said, "Sam, this is it. We have to turn around, or you and I are going to have a pretty bad day, and one hell of a swim back."

Sam looked at his own power monitor. It had moved further towards the left than he'd expected. *Maybe, he'd travelled further than he thought.* He would have to turn around.

"Okay, you turn around. I just want to see what's beyond this bend."

Frank shook his head. "No, we go together or not at all."

"Suit yourself, Frank. We go together then."

"And then, no matter what, we turn around?"

"Agreed," Sam replied.

The dark tunnel appeared to narrow again, giving Sam the worry that he'd been wrong again. No ship could have travelled through such a narrow section. The speed of the current increased again, and the height of the tunnel dropped so much that he had to lean forward to stop his head hitting the ceiling.

As the pull from the powerful current gripped him, Sam realized his mistake. He was never going to make it back against this sort of river flow. Then he came around the corner, and forgot about all his concerns.

In front of him, were the remains of the Mahogany Ship.

Sam could only see part of the bow of the ship, but even that much of it indicated how enormous the grand vessel once was. The stern and main compartments were entirely buried in sand and river silt. Instantly, he realized the reason for the narrowing of the tunnel — the Mahogany Ship had become lodged ahead, and over the last two centuries, become filled with sand and rocks, until the tunnel became nearly completely blocked.

The bow itself was raised above the waterline.

"My God, we found it!" Frank said.

"Of course we did."

"I never doubted you, mate."

"Come on, Frank, now that we're here, we may as well explore it," Sam said, dragging his Seadoo up on the submerged sandy beach.

Frank nodded his head and followed.

Just before the waterline Sam saw the damage. The gash in the massive hull appeared unnatural. As though a single rock had torn through her hull at that precise location, leaving the rest of the beautiful ship unscathed. Sam gave it minimal thought before proceeding to enter through it.

"Are you certain it's the Mahogany Ship?" Frank asked.

"That's what I'm trying to find out."

Sam swam through the dark hull, and past the old ladders, until he reached a cabin above the waterline. Carefully bracing himself on the inner deck, Sam expected its timbers to crumble beneath his weight, but the rare, blackened wood remained strong as steel.

He was certain that it wasn't mahogany, but that didn't matter. Nothing in the notes from the survivors of the Emily Rose, ever determined that it was indeed made out of mahogany, only that it was a blackened wood, unfamiliar to them all.

Against his better judgement, Sam climbed the ladder and stood on top of the now dry inside cabin. It was dark, and the wood seemed unnaturally sound. He removed his facemask and breathed the stale air.

Frank looked at him, waited another minute, before shrugging his shoulders and removing his facemask too. "This ship is hundreds of years old. You sure it's going to take our weight?"

"No clue, but she seems pretty strong to me." Pointing his flashlight to the walkway leading towards the aft of the ship, Sam said, "Shall we?"

"All right, but if this thing starts to break apart, I'm going to be out of here before you can stop me."

"Agreed."

Sam walked confidently over the sturdy floorboards. He'd already guessed why they were in such a good condition, but all the same, he knew he should have been more circumspect about exploring the ancient wreck. They looked down several openings in the walkway. Each appeared empty, all evidence of the original occupants of the vessel now gone.

"Seems deserted," Frank said.

"What did you expect, treasure?"

"Well, yes, actually. We did start this hunt with a gold coin. I kind of expected more of the stuff."

Sam laughed. "Everyone assumes that sunken ships carry gold. In my experience, they normally carry rotten wood, and a myriad of sea life. Here of course, being fresh water, and in an area devoid of light, the ship is just an old ship, and nothing more. I hope Mr. Rodriguez isn't too unhappy with his investment."

"He's a big boy. He'll just be glad that we found her, but he's keen to prove that she was Spanish, and would have been bloody heartbroken if you'd found something that suggested she was not." Frank then looked a solid door at the end of the internal companionway. "What about that?"

"The door?"

The door looked more like something out of Fort Knox than a door on a ship. "Whoever built that wanted to keep something out."

"Or something in?" Sam suggested.

Frank's arms shook suddenly, like a cold shiver. The suggestion appeared to have triggered a nerve, Sam noticed. Then, shrugging the thought off, Frank said, "Nah, something like that there . . . was designed to keep something precious in. I've worked with enough gold in my time to know when I'm close to something of value."

"We'll see."

Sam pushed on the door, but it wasn't going to move. He kicked at it and received the same response.

There was a large keyhole, made of iron, in the middle of the door. The iron had well and truly rusted, leaving more of a hole than lock, which was large enough that he could see through to the contents of the other side of the door.

In an instant, he saw it.

"Holy shit. That's a lot of gold."

Sam paused, studying how the door connected to its frame. Despite the keyhole, the whole thing appeared to be completely molded to the frame surrounding it, as though a team of carpenters were required to open it.

And perhaps there once were?

"You want a hand with that door?" Frank asked.

"Sure, what've you got in mind? I don't think even the two of us would have any hope in knocking it down."

Bringing out a diamond tipped angle grinder, Frank replied, "This."

"Wow. What were you expecting, bringing that?"

"You thought I'd be stupid enough to enter a submerged shipwreck, without a means of cutting my way out if things went wrong? No way, I look after myself."

The story didn't seem to match up, but Sam was glad not to have to return to the dive platform in the Mahogany Cavern before being able to access the locked room.

Minutes later, Frank had cut a hole in the door, large enough for the two of them to shimmy through.

On the back wall of the ship's vaulted room, Sam could see

the remains of a very old treasure chest, now broken open. And inside the dilapidated chest, were at least two hundred gold coins.

Sam stepped forward and picked one up.

It was identical to the others he'd seen. The gold, having lost none of its luster, sparkled as though it were only just minted yesterday.

"Frank, I think we just found the Mahogany Ship."

"That we did, Sam."

Sam carefully looked around the rest of the room. It was almost completely empty, with the exception of the gold coins.

But is it here? Sam thought, disappointed that he hadn't found it yet.

The two explored the room and where they could, accessed the rest of the ship. Nothing indicated that it was even still there, but Sam knew that it was early days yet. For the most part, he had at least found what he and his father had searched for all those years ago.

After a number of hours of searching, it was time to return to the Mahogany Cave. Sam was the first to look at the remaining power on his Seadoo. It was low, but he might make it back. Then again, he might not.

"How much juice have you got in yours, Frank?"

"Enough, maybe. It will be close. I kind of wish we'd brought a reserve power supply."

"My fault. Okay, Frank, you take my battery pack. That way, when yours becomes depleted you'll have mine to fall back on."

Frank looked at Sam's battery monitor, already close to empty. He was a bright man—Sam had no doubt that he could predict the outcome of them both trying to return to the

Mahogany Cave. "Okay, thanks Sam. We'll come back for you as soon as we can."

"Not a problem. I'd like some time alone with this old lady, anyway."

Frank unclipped the power pack and put it in his pocket. With a quick wave of his right arm, the man disappeared, leaving Sam alone, to explore the cold, dark, confines of the ancient ship.

If it's still here, I'll find it.

By the next morning, Sam heard the sounds of the two motorized Seadoos approaching. He waited until they came up from the crack in the hull. Michael Rodriguez' was the first head to pop up through the still water inside the hull, quickly followed by Frank's.

"Morning Sam, I brought you some breakfast," Michael said, handing him two large bacon and egg rolls, filled with barbecue sauce. "I believe congratulations are in order."

"I believe so," Sam said, relieved to see Michael's gregarious face again. The man was obviously driven when he had a purpose, and the search for the Mahogany Ship had kept him going for years. Sam had seen the same look in his own face, when he finally reached the answer to an ancient question, or lost artefact.

He took Michael for a tour of the fabled ship.

"It's going to take some time to recover everything. And you and I both know that there's going to be a lot of red tape around its excavation. But at the end of the day, I think it's safe to say, we found the Mahogany Ship."

"That's great, Sam. Thank you, for everything."

Over the course of the next five days, Sam, Michael and Frank photographed, marked, and examined the entire ship where they could reach, while Byron made reports and documented the information for the world to one day know.

That afternoon, the three of them made the discovery known to the world, via a televised press conference. Michael indicated that the exact location of the fabled ship would remain hidden to protect her from looters, and treasure hunters.

That night, the four men drank expensive whiskey, fine wines, and ate decadent food to celebrate.

After each man had gone to bed, Sam stayed up late, completing some final reports to go with the discovery. Despite finding the Mahogany Ship, he still hadn't found what he was really after. He would remain on site for the next few weeks until he could confirm that it was no longer aboard when the Mahogany Ship disappeared.

And if it was gone, then what hope would humanity have of ever finding them?

Taking a snapshot of the GPS coordinates, Sam looked up the farmers who owned the land. They weren't going to be impressed with all the attention their quiet parcel of land was about to get, now that the discovery of the Mahogany Ship had become national news.

Sam looked at the registered owner of the land on which the mine shaft rested, and then double checked the date of purchase.

I don't believe it!

Sam looked at the old land and council papers again. At the bottom line was the name, Michael Rodriguez and the date of sale, December 3, 1983.

It was the first time that his gut feeling had been confirmed.

Michael's been lying to me, but why?

Metallurgical analysis had already dated the original gold coin to the 15th century, so that much had been true . . . and the wood itself had also come from the 15th century. So if it was a hoax, Michael had gone a long way to preserving it.

He dialed a number to see if his thoughts were right.

It rang three or four times and then a familiar voice answered.

"Aliana, it's good to hear your voice!"

"Samuel, I thought you had left me for another woman . . ."

"Never!" Sam replied, then, quick to get to the point, he said, "Aliana, I have a problem, and I need to pick that fantastic brain of yours."

He went through what he knew to date, finishing with the fact that he had no proof that the entire treasure ship had been a hoax, and neither could he think of a reason why a man like Rodriguez would even want to do so.

"But something's not right, and I need your help to prove it."

"Tell them that you want to bring me in as a scientific name to report on the find, so that the wider community of archeology will see it as legitimate," Aliana suggested.

"But you're a microbiologist. Why do archeologists want to listen to you?"

"Because I can date the microbes that were on the hull of that ship, and where it once came from."

"I hadn't thought of that, of course." Sam pictured her in his arms, and said, "I knew there was a reason I loved you. You're beautiful and incredibly intelligent. When can you get here?"

"I'll pack now, and can have my jet leave tonight—they

won't be happy about the short notice, but that's why I pay them their exorbitant holding fee. I should be there by tomorrow afternoon, your time. It will be just like old times."

Sam's mind flashed back to the night that they had spent together inside a similarly cold, yet beautiful, subterranean cavern, when they found the last airship, the Magdalena The prospect was welcoming.

"I'll see you then. Aliana . . . and yes, I've missed you."

"I've missed you too, Samuel. Keep yourself safe."

"I'm fine. Michael has no reason to hurt me. I just don't understand what this is all about. A part of me still hopes that the ship was real . . . maybe, he had a rough idea where it was and bought up large farming land, just so that he could secure its discovery."

"It seems pretty far-fetched to me, but we'll find out soon enough."

Sam's cell flashed with a message.

He quickly opened it, hoping that Aliana had sent him an additional message.

Instead, he found an online freebee email account name. One of those with about ten numbers after an otherwise normal name like "John," most commonly associated with robot based spam marketing. There was no name attached to the message, and had he tried to ring the number back, his cellular service provider would have informed him that the number was no longer active.

He switched on his laptop, and typed the name of the account into the login page, followed by a password that that was pre-arranged.

There was only one message waiting for him.

SAM,

I'VE TAKEN YOUR COIN TO A NUMISMATICS EXPERT. THE COIN IS LEGIT. ONE PROBLEM THOUGH. IT'S IN MINT CONDITION. IF IT WAS FOUND IN A TREASURE CHEST, LOCKED AWAY IN A CAVE, MAYBE IT COULD BE POSSIBLE. BUT NOT UNDERWATER IN A RIVER. THAT'S IMPOSSIBLE. SOMEONE IS LYING TO YOU. I SUGGEST YOU LOOK AFTER YOURSELF.

ELISE.

CHAPTER 14

The strange blue light seemed to be reflecting off the sarcophagus, and shining directly on it, making it glow a deep blue color. Billie looked at the image of the Mahogany Ship on the wall. It could have been any ship on earth, except this one had eight masts. On its deck, were the simple markings of the Master Builders, and next to them, a scepter with the sun shining out of it.

Her eyes dropped much lower, and saw that Tom was staring at her, breathing deeply, and still gripping the hammer—ready to kill an intruder. He then noticed what she was looking at, and said, "Is that what I think it is?"

"The Mahogany Ship."

"Which means . . ." Realization crossed his face, and he said, "Sam Reilly was here a couple weeks ago and he must have seen it. Why else would he have left, unless he thought that the last real Master Builder was on that ship?"

Billie nodded her head.

"There's something else you need to know, Tom."

"What's that?"

"You and Sam weren't the first people to lay eyes on this

place in the past 1000 years." She looked up at him with expectation in her eyes, "Who else do you know that has gone looking for the Mahogany Ship?"

"Michael Rodriguez!" Tom answered instantly. "Of course he knew about the pyramid. He's mining just below it. He must have any number of geologists who have investigated the area. No wonder he explored it before us, and left it alone — upon discovering no real value inside, he didn't want to lose money by identifying an archeological site right above his largest mine shaft!"

"That's right, but something about this picture made him want to bring Sam Reilly into the equation."

"What makes you so certain that Rodriguez did see this picture before us?"

"Because the likelihood of an oceanic disaster drawing one of five known people in the world who have even heard of the Master Builders, and the only one who'd realized that the Mahogany Ship was connected, is infinitely small. But then to have Rodriguez turn up just after you and Sam dived the site, and ask Sam to help him with a brand new lead on the Mahogany Ship, is just plain impossible."

"You're right. But for what purpose could a man like Rodriguez have to con Sam into exploring a Mayan tomb? I mean, the man's already rich, so what could drive him to such a ruse?"

"He must have needed the credibility that only Sam could provide to his discovery of the Mahogany Ship?"

"But even that doesn't make sense. What could possibly be so valuable to him that he would need such an elaborate hoax to drag Sam into it?"

"No, not money — he has that. Something infinitely more important to him . . ."

"What's more important than money to a rich man?"

"Power."

"Oh, shit!"

"What?"

"I just remembered where I've seen Rodriguez previously . . . I know exactly why he needed him . . . Sam's walking into a trap! Come on, we have to get back to the dive bell so we can get a message through to Sam!"

Sam left the cavern, alone in the middle of the night.

Leaving without anyone noticing, he slid into the water. He allowed the diving scooter to submerge below the surface, silently, until he was 300 feet along the tunnel before switching on the electrical motor.

He followed the tunnel for more than an hour before he reached it.

Looking upon the hull of the Mahogany Ship, he smiled. They had done an exceptional job at making the fake exceedingly realistic, but they'd forgot about one simple thing.

Science.

The dead barnacles would give them away. Sam chiseled at the wooden hull, catching fragments of the dead organic matter in a glass container. He then moved inside and repeated the process. It wasn't until he dug away at the sand burying the middle of the ship that he found immediate proof.

After digging through six feet of soft, dry, sand, Sam struck something hard. He cleared away more sand, until he started to get an idea of what he had run into. It took almost an hour before he could see it clearly, and when he did, he knew he was in trouble.

Concrete.

The entire ship was bolted onto enormous concrete blocks, confirming that his entire search had been for nothing, or worse—for Michael Rodriguez's gain. *But for what gain?*

It was then that he noticed that he was being watched.

"Rodriguez..." Sam turned to face him.

The man ran. With his dive mask and SCUBA equipment still fully attached, he was able to dive straight through the hole in the hull.

Sam chased after him, grabbing his dive mask only and trying to free dive the thirty-odd feet to where both their Seadoos rested on the sand.

Ahead of him, the whirl of the unknown man's propulsion system stirred up the water with silt from the river's bed.

Sam could have returned to the fake Mahogany Ship and grabbed the rest of his equipment, but it would take too much time. Instead, he attached the Seadoo's air tube, placed it directly in his mouth to breathe from, and kept going.

The masked man had already gained a couple minutes head start on him.

He tried his best to cut the corners of the tunnel, but so did the other man. By the time he reached the dive platform at the Mahogany Cavern, Sam could see the man already climbing onto the mine shaft elevator.

Shit, I'm too late.

Sam slowly climbed the ladder and stood on the dive platform. Thirty-odd feet above him, he could now clearly see Michael Rodriguez aboard the elevator.

Michael stopped the elevator. "Sorry, Sam. You're one hell of a guy, but you just wouldn't let it go, would you? I mean, I was keen for you to get all the rewards and accolades associated with this discovery. Hell you could have kept the Spanish treasure. No one would have ever realized that I planted it all here. Do you know how much eight hundred 15th century Spanish gold coins are worth? But no, you fucked it up by discovering the truth, didn't you?"

"And what is the truth? I don't understand — as you said, the cost of the old Spanish treasure must outweigh any possible benefit of being acclaimed as the discoverer of the Mahogany Ship?" Sam already knew his fate — he was going to die here, but he needed to know why. And for every minute he kept his new-found psychopath talking, he would have a chance of finding a solution.

"Now . . . now . . . you've been watching too many James Bond movies . . . this isn't the part where the villain tells Bond his evil plans just before leaving him to die."

"But that's what you're going to do to me, isn't it?"

"Here? Yes . . . you're going to have to die here."

"Then why not tell me? Let me know what I'm dying for."

"I like you Sam. I was honest when I told you that we could be great friends — so I'll let you in on a secret. Let's just say that by proving the Mahogany Ship came from Spain, I can prove my birthright to something far more valuable than the richest mine in the world. Good day, Mr. Reilly."

With that said, Michael pressed the green elevator button and disappeared above him, leaving Sam alone in the vast cavern.

CHAPTER 15

Bendigo airport had one runway, and even it was comprised entirely of dirt. At the end of the runway, as the small Regional Express plane took off, a single woman remained on her own. Wearing hiking boots, she appeared tall—six feet at least, with blonde hair and a slim figure.

Aliana fretted.

It was not like her, but something in her gut told her that Sam was in trouble.

Left alone at the end of the dirt runway of the outback country airport, Aliana wondered if she'd made the right decision when she decided not to bring her private jet. *No, it's never a good idea to show your hand to an enemy.* She'd prudently taken a regional carrier's flight out to the small country town.

It wasn't like her to worry, but neither was it like Sam to forget about her. There was no reason to think the worst—Michael had specifically requested Sam's help. Whatever was going on here, the man had wanted Sam. Still, she couldn't help recall the last words that Sam had said to her—*someone is lying, I just don't know why.*

By the time it was dark, Aliana called Sam's cell for the fifth time, and someone picked up.

"Hello, Sam Reilly's phone?" The man's voice was confident, like someone used to being in charge.

"Hi, can I speak to Sam?"

She thought she could hear the man sigh on the other side of the cell. "I'm sorry, what did you say your name was?"

"Aliana. I was supposed to be coming to Bendigo to help Sam with his project."

"Oh . . . gotcha . . ." the man on the other end of the phone, sighed again. "You must be his girlfriend. I'm so sorry to tell you this . . . Sam's been involved in an accident."

"Sam's dead!"

"No, no, we sure hope not. We had a cave in, and Sam was on the wrong side of the tunnel at the time. We have a team working around the clock to remove the debris. We're all pretty confident he'll be fine. I wouldn't fly out here until it's all sorted. It might take us a few days, that's all. When were you thinking of coming out?"

"I already did."

"You did? My goodness, you should have told me. I'll come to the airport myself to pick you up."

Aliana felt something uneasy in her stomach and replied, "It's okay. You must be very busy. Maybe I should just grab a room at a motel and wait for word that Sam's all right?"

"No way—I wouldn't hear of it. I'll be at the airport in half an hour. Wait right there."

The large silver six-wheeled Mercedes pulled up alongside the entrance to the airport. Despite the ostentatious truck, the man who climbed out appeared to Aliana like a down-to-earth, honest, mine worker. He wore denim pants with no label, a polo shirt, and rugged boots. The only sign of his billionaire background was the Rolex on his wrist, but even that could have been a fake.

"Aliana Wolfgang?" The man asked politely.

"That's me." She smiled.

"Michael Rodriguez." He offered his hand, and then said, "I'm really sorry you had to find out about Sam this way. We're really are hoping to have him out in the next couple days. Don't you worry—he has plenty of supplies on his side of the tunnel. He'll be all right, just you watch."

Aliana shook his hand, and then climbed up into the small truck. Michael then began to drive south and out of town. The two spoke on the way to the mine site, and she quickly found herself naturally at ease with him. There was something about Rodriguez that she couldn't help but trust. He seemed like the real deal somehow, despite what Sam had discovered about the Mahogany Ship. She could see why Sam was stuck for an explanation about the lie.

Once they reached the mine's entrance Michael showed her on the map of the tunnel exactly where the cave-in was, and what they were doing to release him.

Aliana asked, "Is there anything I can do to help?"

"There's nothing more to do, I'm afraid. My men have it under control, and they should have him out in the next four to five hours. Is there anything I can do for you, while you wait?"

Aliana looked at his face. It was kind and reassuring. "No thanks. I have some of the information that Sam provided me about your discovery of the Mahogany Ship, I liked to take a look while I wait. Is there anywhere I can plug in my laptop?"

"Of course, I'll have one of my men free some space in the computer tent."

"Thanks." Aliana looked at him for a moment longer and then said, "I really mean that. For everything. Thank you."

Michael took her hand in his and replied, "You're welcome. This will be over before you know it."

The hours passed quickly as Aliana made a list of questions to ask Sam regarding the Mahogany Ship. There seemed to be more discrepancies in the details of the find than she first realized, and Aliana was starting to wonder if there was some truth in what Sam had said to her.

Maybe Michael isn't entirely what he seems?

By eleven p.m. Michael came into her tent and said, "Look, we're doing all that we can, and my team will keep doing so through the night, but it appears that it will take much longer than we first anticipated. I've arranged a room for you at a local motel. Why don't you spend the night there?"

"I'd like to help," she persisted.

"I'm sure you would, but there's very little you can do at this moment. I'll come pick you up first thing in the morning."

She hated the thought of it, but knew that he had a point. Nothing could be gained by waiting at the tunnel's side. "Okay, sure . . . but promise you'll ring me the second you're through."

"Of course."

Michael then insisted on driving her back to town, himself. After he left, she had a simple dinner and then relaxed in the bath. Despite being on her own private jet, the long flight and recent knowledge about Sam's accident had taken its toll on her body.

She decided to go to bed early. Her head had only just rested on the uncomfortable pillow, before she rolled over twice and then fell sound asleep.

And then there was a knock at the door.

Aliana pulled the curtain back and then opened the door. She paused a mere second before throwing her arms around the man on the other side

"Mr. Reilly, I can't believe you're here!"

The older man wrapped his strong arms around her, comforting her, and then replied, "Call me James, darling. You're the first girl my Sam has ever brought to see his old man. That makes you practically family."

Aliana stood back and looked at the man's face again. Although she could imagine that he had a ruthless streak, it looked kindly at her now. James shared the same piercing grey-blue eyes and confident smile that she recognized in Sam.

"It's so good to see you here. I think Sam's in trouble."

James smiled kindly at her and then said, "How about I come in, and you tell me what you're doing here."

She explained everything that had happened and finished by telling him about the mine collapse. She described how Michael had been very good to her, but that she worried he might not be telling the entire truth about all he was doing to help Sam survive.

"Did they tell you that's where Sam's mine shaft had caved in?" James asked.

"Yeah, they've been working frantically for 12 hours now to try and reach him, at a place about ten miles south of town."

"Really, that's funny. I would have thought that they'd have better luck tunneling where they left him."

"What do you mean, left him?" Aliana just about screamed the words. Then, fumbling through a map on the table in front of her, said, "This was where he disappeared."

"No it wasn't . . . that place is more than fifty miles away, where they left him."

"How can you know that?"

"Look, my son can be a self-righteous, altruistic ass at times, with no care for himself or the family fortune. But stupid, he certainly is not. He and I looked for the Mahogany Ship years ago. Came mighty close to finding her, too. Sam knew immediately, that Michael was lying, but hoped that somehow we'd missed something years ago. Either way, he never trusted Michael, and so he left a GPS beacon at the entrance of the mine shaft and asked me to keep an eye on things. I own several satellites for just such spying . . ."

"So, if Sam's not trapped down below this mine shaft where Michael took me, what happened to him?"

"That, I don't know." James took out a large smartphone from his pocket and clicked on a GPS app. "Here, this is what the mine shaft where Sam's been working looked like three days ago."

At first glance, Aliana thought it looked more like the entrance to a bomb shelter, left over from the Cold War.

"And, this is what it looks like now."

The image clearly displayed a small mountain with cleared soil, and no evidence of what was once the entrance to the mineshaft.

"So, you're saying they've most likely bulldozed the entrance to one of the largest underground water cave systems in Australia, while he was deep inside it?"

"Yes."

Aliana's usually carefree smile was crestfallen.

"I wouldn't worry too much," James said, comforting her with his arms. "I think you will find that my Sam is much harder to kill than that, and an expert cave diver, he will find another way out, or at least manage to keep himself alive until we can make one."

James, she noticed, never seemed too worried about his son. But the sheer fact that he was here demonstrated that he loved him very much, and was willing to do anything required to protect him.

"I still don't even understand why Rodriguez would want to hurt Sam. I mean, it was Sam who proved that he'd discovered the final resting place of The Mahogany Ship?"

"Only he didn't, did he?"

"What do you mean, he didn't?" She fidgeted with a cup of coffee. "He found the Spanish gold, and everything carbon dated to the 15th century."

"I don't know where the Spanish gold came from—it was probably a cleverly executed and expensive exercise in deception, and for what purpose, I don't yet know. I do, however, know that the Mahogany Ship settled nowhere near this location."

"How could you possibly be so sure?"

"Because Sam and I once looked for her together, and that's not even close to where she was."

"So you found her?"

"No, but I have an accurate account of the journey of one Mr. Jack Robertson, who survived the sinking of the Emily Rose in 1812. They were the first settlers to discover the Mahogany Ship, and their journey from Warrnambool to Sydney Cove never came close to Bendigo."

Aliana interrupted. "Yes, but that's all common knowledge. What isn't known is where, exactly, they spotted the Mahogany Ship."

"As I was saying, young Aliana . . ." James patiently began, as though he were speaking to a small child. "I have an accurate account of the journey of Mr. Jack Robertson. In it, there is a very specific, and detailed description of the route they took, and even the longitude and latitude where they were when they spotted that damn ship."

"So you do know where it is?"

"My dear Dr. Wolfgang, this may take some time to explain if you keep interrupting."

"I'm sorry, James. Do go on."

"No, we only have the location where the party of survivors were when they first saw the Mahogany Ship. Sam and I reached the location, but all remnants of the Mahogany Ship nearby had either been destroyed, burned, or removed entirely. The ship herself, although interesting, was of minimal concern to me. It was what she was carrying that had particularly inflicted me with a keen interest."

"What was she carrying?" Aliana asked, more confused now than she'd been when she first started talking to Sam about the Mahogany Ship possibly being a giant, expensive, hoax.

"A powerful scepter, called the 'The Ark of Light,' which, legend has it, held the ability to focus natural sunlight with extreme precision, or 'Entrap Ra, the Sun God' so that he might destroy one's enemies. The crux of the matter being that the Ark was a very powerful weapon."

"And that was what you were after?"

"Yes, and I believe that it, too, is the most likely reason for which our friend Michael Rodriguez has gone to such lengths to orchestrate bringing us all here."

Aliana wanted to scream in frustration.

Each answer seemed to lead to another two questions.

"Why would Michael, a billionaire, want an ancient weapon?"

James smiled idiotically, at the simple question, and offered the possible explanation, "It's a very good weapon?"

"That's bullshit. A man like Rodriguez could afford his own Army, Navy, and Air Force. So why would he care about a weapon that had the ability to destroy things with bolts of fire and lightning?"

"Because, legend has it, that as well as being a tremendous weapon, the Ark of Light — when held at the top of the Pyramid of Giza at midday of the winter solstice — pointed directly to The Tomb of Knowledge. A place buried by the passing of a number of Ice Ages, it has been said that the place was created by God himself, as a means of storing all knowledge of man."

She studied his face. It was passionate to the point of obsession. "And why do you want to find such a place?"

"Because knowledge, my dear, is power. And power, like any drug, never seems to be quite sufficient for one's needs."

Aliana shook her head in wonder.

She could see so much of Sam in this old man, despite his affliction with a number of vices, including, and not limited to greed, lust, and grandiose misalignment. Yet, he had the same attractive looks in a rogue kind of style as his son, and a charm that was hard not to enjoy.

"Okay, so if Rodriguez is after this Ark, why drag you and Sam into it?"

"That's simple. He needs what we have, to find it."

"And what do you have?"

"A map of where the scepter was taken after it left the

Mahogany Ship."

"Are you fucking serious? You have such a map? Why didn't you just use it in the first place, find the stupid scepter and go and get your unlimited power?"

"Because there's a catch . . ."

"Of course there is." Aliana decided she hadn't met a more infuriating person.

"The map depicts the scepter buried in a cave twenty-two miles, precisely, north of where the Mahogany Ship was left. There are a number of other markers used to identify the treasure, but the most important of all markers, is the exact location of the Mahogany Ship. Mr. Robertson made certain that it would never be found by accident, and when he returned to retrieve the Ark, he attempted to destroy the ship by burning it. Years later, when others came across the ship, it was found blackened — thus the mistaken presumption that the ship was built of the dark mahogany."

"So, if Mr. Robertson returned for the Ark, wouldn't it now be somewhere else?"

"No. You see, as luck would have it for you and me, Jack Robertson had a rather criminal past. And he was about to pay for a crime he'd committed more than twenty years earlier, while still living in England," James said. "The story goes, Jack, once a highwayman and murderer, had been paid by Lord Dickson Mills, one of the richest men in England at the turn of the 19th century, to murder his wife, Mary, who he'd suspected had been having an affair. Only when Jack shot the woman, in cold blood, he realized that he had entered the wrong room, very nearly killing the man's daughter, Lady Rose, instead. Like a fool, he'd stayed to try and save the young girl's life, until someone came and he was forced to flee for his life."

"That's some history. Is that why he left for Australia, to escape?"

"Yes, before he was hanged. Now, when he left aboard the Emily Rose, a man by the name of John Langham followed. This was the man who was having an affair with Lady Mary Mills. Feeling responsible, the man had made a vow to hunt down the man and bring him to justice—and justice meant death. Through unknown and unlikely events, Jack Robertson, John Langham and Dawson Mills, Lord Mill's only son, were the only three survivors of the wreckage of the Emily Rose who would ever reach Sydney Cove. Of the three, only John realized their strange past connection. On his death bed, he wrote to Rose asking her for forgiveness for failing in his promise to avenge her, and describing how he'd come to forgive the man who had injured her."

"Lady Rose was less than forgiving?"

"Exactly, Lady Rose, now grown up, and having survived both her parents and her brother, had little left in her life than to kill the man whom she'd imagined had taken them all away from her. Having inherited a fortune, she sailed to the foundling Australia, and followed Jack until he reached his treasure. There, she killed him. In a strange whim, Jack had cut the raft which housed the Ark and let the treasure disappear into the tunnel forever."

Aliana, engrossed by the sad story, looked up and asked, "How did you come by so much of this history?"

"Because Lady Rose looked at the treasure map that Jack had been carrying on him. Three leather parts, stitched together and marked John, Jack, and Dawson—the three names of the survivors of the Emily Rose. Men whose lives were destined to be entwined in love and hatred. She couldn't believe it. She took it home, and never told anyone about any of it, until, on her own deathbed, she wrote it all down, with the inclusion of the map."

"But how did you come to learn of it?"

James then opened a plastic folder, which showed the old map, worn, but still intact. "This map, my great, great grandmother found, after she killed Jack Robertson."

Aliana's cell phone rang.

She looked down at it — a private number — and answered, "Aliana speaking."

"Aliana, we just got Sam out!" She recognized Rodriguez's voice. "I'm coming by now to pick you up."

"That's great! Thanks."

Aliana then looked at James, "Now, how do you want to do this?"

James grabbed the keys to an old, beat up, Holden Utility. "Come on, I better take you to my place."

James was just starting to enjoy his new ride, a 1970s Holden Utility. Noticeable less flashy than what he was used to, it was built before the Environmental Protection Agencies got hold of the motor industry, and it came equipped with an 8-cylinder, 6-liter, leaded petrol engine — all power, and no handling.

Sam, he knew, would hate it.

Around ten miles out of town, he got out to open the gate so that he could drive into the farm where he was staying. An old, 1890 homestead rested on the hill at the end of the dirt road. Its roof, rusty corrugated iron, and its walls built of rock and timber, it had obviously seen better days. He had no doubt he was the first to rent it in more than a decade. James looked at Aliana, "This is my place."

"You've been staying here?"

"Of course. Why, don't you think I can do it tough?"

"Sure, I don't doubt you could—but it's not your normal style, is it?" she said

James laughed at that. "My son's told you a bit about me, hasn't he?" She nodded her head. "Well, I might like a somewhat decadent lifestyle these days, but you'd be surprised what I've lived through to get here."

Judging by her face, James thought Aliana most likely would have been very much surprised. He parked the car and the two walked up the old sandstone steps and into the house.

Inside, the house looked entirely unlived in. Covers were still over the furniture, and a pile of dust seemed to cover the entire place.

James opened up his laptop, and said, "Here's the current satellite picture of the entrance to the mine."

The steel hatch, seen in previous images, was now covered with soil and fresh grass had been laid over the top of it, making it literally disappear.

"At least they've left the place alone," she said, her voice soft. "We should be able to get through easily enough. They never would have filled the hole. Michael will want to return for his gold, at some stage—it shouldn't be too hard to find him."

"Don't get too excited. Look over there," James pointed to the camouflaged Armored Patrol Vehicle, nearly buried in a ditch no more than fifty feet from the entrance to the shaft.

Her eyes were despondent, but not beaten.

"What did you expect? Michael's got more than ten million dollars' worth of Spanish gold down there. He's not going to leave it around for just anyone."

"So, now what? Can we destroy that APC?"

"We could do that . . ." James smiled, as though he was genuinely considering it. "I think I have a better idea, one which won't give away our hand quite so much. A slow win is sometimes more satisfying."

"And what's that?"

"We're going to rescue my son, and then we're going to steal Michael's treasure."

"Now you're talking . . ."

"And after that, we're going to make Michael pay by beating him to his ambition."

"How are we going to do that?"

"By locating the real Mahogany Ship."

Alana looked at the topographical map of the surrounding area. "That tunnel is almost 500 feet below the surface, we're going to need a lot more equipment to rescue Sam . . ."

"That's already covered."

"What's your plan?"

At that moment, the window sill started to vibrate as the ground shook, and despite the pale blue sky outside, the sound of thunder could be heard.

James smiled and stepped outside.

An enormous military helicopter approached, the twin rotors of the Chinook turning the dry land into a dust storm.

"And here come our reinforcements."

Tom shut down the engine, and casually stepped out of the helicopter. He looked at James Reilly sitting on the front porch of a big old homestead, a local beer in his hand and a beautiful blonde by his side. The old man had a smile on his face that radiated sheer delight. It could have been the company of the beautiful woman next to him, or the fact that he was on an adventure with real value for the first time in years.

It took a second for Tom to recognize the stunning creature as Aliana. He hadn't expected her to be there. No one had told him that she knew anything about this.

"It's good to see you again, Aliana," Tom said, as he kissed her on the cheek.

Throwing her long, slender body around him with a solid embrace, she replied, "You have no idea how good it is to see you here. Thanks for coming."

"You're welcome. If I'd known that you were stuck here, alone with this man, I would have come to your rescue sooner."

"Hey, don't you think for a second that I can't hear you, Tom," James said. "You want a beer?"

"I'm only kidding, James. Sure, I'll have a beer." Tom grinned mischievously, "Have you found Sam, yet?"

Aliana, brought up the satellite display of the now covered mine shaft, "This is what remains of the mineshaft, and this is an image nearly 50 miles away, where they say that they were working when Sam disappeared. So, it's safe to say that this is where he is," she said pointing to the now hidden hatch. "What we don't know is how we're going to get him out of there."

"On my flight from Los Angeles here, I had time to look at the maps of the tunnels that Sam had already made. I've then superimposed those with the land above, based on this topographical map." Tom opened up the satellite images of the surrounding landscapes. "As you can see, there is very little in the way of rivers above ground anywhere near here, but if you travel 60 miles north, you can see the Dharuk river flows strong for hundreds of miles and then seems to just disappear into the side of a mountain. As we all know, rivers have to go somewhere. When you look at Sam's underground maps, you can see that this third tunnel, the largest of the five mapped underground waterways that he's explored, it appears to keep coming from the north. That's less than 10 miles from the end of where his initial search reached."

"We still have no way of knowing that those two rivers are one and the same," James pointed out.

"Not certain, but look at this." Tom clicked another button, and a third image joined the picture. This one was created using prediction software, designed to determine future sizes of the flow of water, based on previous size and strength.

"They're the same river!" Aliana agreed.

"Either that, or just a very close neighbor," James acknowledged.

"Just one question," Aliana said.

"What's that?" Tom replied.

"How are we going to bridge that 10-mile gap?"

"That's simple . . . I wasn't sure how far we were going, so I brought the MOLE."

CHAPTER 16

The small team arrived at the edge of the Dharuk River early the following morning. Aliana watched as Tom drove the mole out of the back of the enormous helicopter. To her, it looked more like something a kid would draw to highlight a bad science fiction story or cover of an eighties era comic book. At the front of the vehicle, a large tunneling device gave it the strange appearance of the nose of a mole, whereas the large tank tracks, reaching the same distance below and above the machine, gave it the odd appearance of large claws. Two windows built inside the tank tracks were the only signs that people might actually be able to fit inside the machine.

Aliana was surprised by how silently it ran, being electrically powered for underwater use. Tom then advised her that the device was capable of floating and submarining in water, and could tunnel through significant amounts of rock.

"What do you think of my girl?" Tom asked.

"I'd say, by the looks of her, that you have an interesting taste in women."

Tom unlocked and then opened the watertight trunk of the mole. A small armory appeared, including plastic explosives and four high powered handguns equipped with silencers.

James' left eyebrow raised in surprise, "You take those on a lot of diving trips with my boy, do you?"

"I wasn't taking any chances, this time."

James took the first Glock out, removed the silencer, emptied the cartridge, and then replaced the rounds, before adeptly reassembling it again. "Looks okay." He then pointed it at an old tin can, forty feet away, and fired five rounds. "Seems to fire straight," he said.

Tom walked towards the remains of the rusty old can. There were four holes all in a grouping no more than a couple inches in total. "Four out of five isn't bad, James." Tom said. "I'm impressed."

James confidently walked up to him and snatched the can out of his hand. Holding it up to the sunlight he pointed out that the fifth shot was so close to the fourth that it almost went through the exact same hole — the tiniest of marks on the side of the hole indicating that it was indeed hit by the fifth bullet.

"Five out of five. Just wait till I tell Sam his old man's a better shot. You can shoot, that's for sure," Tom said.

James scrunched up his face, like he was ready to hit someone.

"Of course I can shoot. I've been a dedicated Republican all my life," James replied, as though that explained everything.

"Talking about weapons, what do you know about Billie?" Tom asked.

"Billie?"

"Billie Swan. The marine archeologist."

"Oh Bill! She and Sam have a history . . ."

"You mean they dated?"

"No, it's much more complex than that. With dating you

sometimes have the chance of one day getting married and then hopefully later getting divorced. What Billie and Sam have is something more definite. Why do you ask?"

"She brought a high powered pistol and silencer to the Mayan site we discovered in the Gulf of Mexico."

James smiled. "I knew I liked that girl."

"Yes, well she decided not to kill me, so it begs the question, why did she take it in the first place?"

"I have an idea about that, but I think Sam could better explain it."

Aliana stood up from the log she'd been sitting on. A half-eaten apple in her hand, Aliana decided she'd heard enough. "Are we going to go find Sam or wait around talking about him?"

"Good point, Aliana," James said, "Rodriguez and his men might just go down the mineshaft, any minute now, having likely guessed that you were on to him."

"That's great," Tom said, pulling out a rocket launcher from the back of the mole. "So we can expect company down there."

The heavy mole floated surprisingly well, considering it more closely resembled a tank than a boat. Displayed along the front steel wall, two monitors displayed both the digital imaging from outside as though it were a windscreen, and on the other side, radar and high frequency sonar images.

Tom adeptly steered the craft using the pedals, like those on an aircraft, with his feet to move the rudder that dragged behind the craft. Each hand gripped the individual throttle controlling the left and right tank tracks.

"Everyone have their seatbelts on?" he asked.

Aliana double checked her five-point seatbelt, and the said, "Are you expecting us to need them?"

Tom smile reassuringly. "Not at all, just a safety kind of guy, that's all."

The pace of the river picked up speed as the mole approached the opening to the cave system. Sitting next to Tom, Aliana leaned forward and asked, "How sure are you that we're not just about to go off some sort of waterfall?"

James gripped her shoulder from behind and warmly said, "Oh, he doesn't, but it's reasonably unlikely, wouldn't you say, Tom?"

"It's all right Aliana. I've taken into account the possible differences in depth of the river. There's less than ten feet of movement between this river and the subterranean river system from Sam's map," Tom said.

"And what if we're wrong about these two rivers being one and the same?"

"Then, we're in trouble," James said, sardonically.

Tom threw the tank tracks into reverse, slowing their progression down the river to a meagre crawl, and said, "Don't worry, we'll be safe."

Entering the dark cave system, Tom flicked on the massive overhead LEDs, flooding the entire area with light. Small ripples flittered where the river approached the end of the large cave, before turning a slight corner and then disappearing into an unknown world.

Moving forward at a crawling pace, Tom had an ominous feeling he knew just where that water at the end of the tunnel was disappearing to. "Anyone want to guess where our river just went?"

He could see whites of Aliana's knuckles as she gripped the

stability bar hard in front of her. "I have an idea I'm not going to like it!"

And then the mole lurched forward, as it entered the first set of rapids.

Skipping over the smaller rapids as they approached the end of the tunnel and slicing through the larger ones, the current picked up considerable pace, until Tom was forced to leave the tank tracks idling. The tracks were no longer able to produce enough force to overcome the flow of the river, leaving them bounding down the river, mostly out of control, like a heavy raft.

At the end of the river, the tunnel veered sharply to the left and the ride become more violent, as the entire river turned white with froth, causing the mole to bob up and down in rapids as large as five feet high.

At its narrowest point ahead, the river was surging and plunging down the inside of the mountain. "Here comes that waterfall you were asking about," Tom said. "Hold on everyone!"

The mole dropped five feet into the first rock pool with a giant splash as the entire craft became submerged before bobbing out to the surface again.

Out the window to his left, Tom could see that the mole was only just floating above the surface of the whitewash. It floated there for a few seconds, being pulled slightly backwards by the flow of water pouring in behind them, before becoming caught in the downward hydraulic of the river, and pulled off the next ledge.

James laughed, like a kid on a ride, "Here we go again!"

The mole dropped off the second into another rock pool. This time, the unnatural flow of the large river spun the mole around in a clockwise motion.

By the fifth revolution, they slammed into the rock at the edge of the pool. In an instant, Tom shoved the two throttles forwards, sending the tank tracks spinning, until they met traction on the rock and sent the mole shooting up and over the next drop.

Tom felt the entire contents of his stomach reach his head, as they free-dived into the deep pool of water at least ten feet below.

Slamming into the deep water, the mole's giant drilling nose acted like a high diver's hands as it broke the surface tension, before submerging nearly twenty feet below.

The mole popped its head above the water again, and started to gently drift down the river at a leisurely pace. James unbuckled his seatbelt, laughing like a demon as he leaned forward, and said, "That was great fun. Let's go do it again!"

Tom shook his head in wonder. Some people don't even know when to be scared. Aliana, on the other hand, looked as though she might spew all over the mole, but was purposely forcing herself to sit up and take in her surroundings.

"How you doing?" he said, looking at her.

"Fine . . . Are we done with the rollercoaster yet?"

"Almost. According to this, we should be just about to meet up with the part of the river where Sam has surveyed." The river, now gradually moving forward with no ripples or violent waves, looked like it went on forever. "Is this a more agreeable pace for you?"

"Much, thank you," she replied.

Tom left the tracks spinning slowly in a forward momentum, just enough to keep them facing forward as they drifted down the river.

Up ahead, the river appeared to just cease.

But rivers never end in a tunnel; they end in the ocean or large inland lakes.

"Can anyone see where the river goes after this?"

James casually buckled his seatbelt again. "I thought you said you had a map?"

"It might have been just a little wrong," Tom replied.

"How wrong?" Aliana asked, worried that although there were no ripples, the current seemed to be increasing again.

"Wrong enough that I only have one guess where all this water is disappearing to."

They were nearing the end of the river, and the flow was fast—like when it was about to drop off the edge of something.

Tom now recognized the distant sound of constant thunder up ahead.

"Hold on everyone."

Just before dropping off the end of the river into the unknown below, Tom pulled on a lever above his head, and the doors to the air ballast opened to full. The heavy mole sank, like a giant stone, as he pushed throttles fully forward again.

Down, down, the mole submerged. In front of him, Tom read the depth gauge reach 80 feet, before he saw what he was looking for.

An opening appeared at the base of the deep tunnel—too small to accommodate the vastness of the river. There, most of the water toppled over the top of the large rock face, whereas some still flowed below it.

The tank tracks reached the gravel bottom with a jolt and kicked the mole into life as it started to drive along the bottom of the river.

"Think skinny thoughts!" Tom said, as he lined up both tank

tracks to drive straight through the hole.

A loud thud could be heard as the mole's tank tracks smashed through the rocky edge of the opening, and then they were out the other side. Above them, the sound of the waterfall, now on their side of the 80-foot rock, could still be heard hammering the water above them.

Tom drove confidently along the now completely submerged river system. "Ah, now, we're in the same subterranean river that Sam mapped earlier."

An hour later, the small team looked through the clear bulletproof dome above their heads to see the remains of a mining platform inside an enormous cavern.

"This must be what Sam said was called the Mahogany Cavern. Up there you can see the dive platform they were working on."

"Are you sure they're still out?" Aliana asked, noticing the lights within the cavern were still running.

"Pretty sure, but don't worry. — we'll be ready if they come," James said.

Tom drove further downwards, towards the exit tunnel.

The tunnel was longer than he'd imagined it, and for a moment Tom worried that he'd taken the wrong one. But then the depth of the tunnel started to decrease, until the tank tracks above their heads were occasional scratching on the ceiling of the tunnel.

The mole slowed, and then, like a four-wheel drive starting to become bogged in the mud, the tank tracks seemed to be turning at a rate faster than they were moving.

"You want me to get out and push?" James asked.

"Not just yet," Sam replied. He pulled the lever above his head, which opened up every air compartment available, causing the mole to become extremely negatively buoyant.

The tank tracks instantly sunk deeper into the sandy bottom with a heavy crunch and began catching again. And then they were through to the other side.

Where the Mahogany Ship waited for them.

They approached the Mahogany Ship from the side, and quickly saw the large hole in its side, where Sam had been entering her bow. Aliana stared out the porthole to her right, where the ship stood. "Tom, you know what Sam would have used when he was diving here. Any sign of his equipment?"

"Not yet. I haven't seen anything. And seeing nothing can often be a good thing when we're talking about searching for a lost cave diver."

"Sam's not drowned," James interrupted, frustration clearly displayed on his face. "There were a number of caverns full of air, and pockets of air throughout the tunnels on the way in here. There's no way Sam could have drowned here. Heck, I bet the athletic bastard, could have managed the trip we just made, holding his breath between the underwater sections."

The statement was ridiculous, but Aliana was grateful for his reassurance.

"Now what do we do then?" she asked.

"We have a look at Rodriguez's fake Mahogany Ship, and take his gold!" James's eyes lit up with excitement.

"What about Sam?" Aliana asked, feeling as though she were the only person capable of staying focused on their primary mission—to save Sam.

"If I know Sam, he would have taken the same route out that we just took to come in," James said.

"Then why didn't we see him?" she argued.

Tom switched both tank track electric motors to off, parking the Mole, and then suggested, "Maybe he was already out?"

"Not likely. We would have seen some sign of him at the river," Aliana said.

"Come on, let's get the gold," James pestered, with a big, stupid grin.

"Are you serious?" Aliana's eyes stared at him.

"If Sam did escape, he would have left a note or something for us on board the Mahogany Ship. Besides, I'd really like to see to what lengths Rodriguez has gone to bring us here."

"All right," Aliana said, "but only so we can see if Sam left us anything to go on. Then we're back to searching for him."

"Agreed."

At the rear of the vehicle was a small airlock chamber, large enough to allow just one person at a time to exit the mole, in full dive gear.

James was the first to leave, followed by Aliana, and Tom agreed to stay and keep guard. If Rodriguez and his men came back while the other two were away, he said he would run them over with the mole at best, and at worst, block the entrance to the Mahogany Ship so that the others could escape.

By the time Aliana climbed through the opening in the ship, and reached the sandy area where the dozen or more footprints indicated others had been entering, she found James's hand, reaching down to help her up.

"Thanks," she said.

"Not a problem."

"Any luck?"

"Yeah, I found it!" James said, showing her a number of

Rodriguez's gold coins. "This is going to really piss him off."

"What about Sam?"

"No idea. How about you have a quick look, and I'll load up the Mole."

"You're unbelievable James!" she said, deciding to look around the ship herself.

"Thanks," James said, as he put his dive mask back on his face and dropped back into the water with a bag full of gold coins.

Aliana then looked through the first few rooms, quickly making certain that Sam wasn't there, lying injured or worse — dead — before moving on to the next ones. It didn't take her long to clear every room in the ship capable of being easily accessed.

At the back of the ship, she saw that a large amount of sand had intentionally been removed. Shining her flashlight on it, she immediately saw how Sam finally determined the Mahogany Ship had been a fake.

The massive wall of concrete had been buried with no more than a few feet of sand, to give the image of the back half of the ship being filled with sand.

It was time to go. Nothing more could be achieved by walking around the fake shipwreck.

"We're out of here," she said to James, who was hurriedly shoving the last of the gold coins in another big bag.

"Okay, can you give me a hand with the second bag? I think I might have overloaded it, and I'd hate to leave Rodriguez with one of his coins."

Not bothering to get into another fight with the man, she picked the smaller of the two bags, and returned to the mole.

After the water was expelled from the diving hatch, Tom

helped her out of her dive gear, and then said, "I'm afraid, this is where the rescue mission ends."

"Why, what's wrong?"

"See the power gauge? We're down to 65 percent."

"So, can't we wait until it gets to 50 percent?"

"No, it's going to draw a lot more power to get back up those rapids," Tom said. "Don't worry. We'll come back for him."

Four hours later, the three were back on the surface, and Tom drove the mole back to the helicopter, ready to be unloaded. Aliana listened as James started whistling a happy tune to himself, while loading the several bags of gold Spanish coins into a safe aboard the helicopter.

"Damn it, James, you're enjoying this, aren't you?"

He stopped whistling and replied, "And why shouldn't I be? Traversing a grade six black water run, in a cross between a tank and a submarine, while stealing gold from a rich asshole — and you know that gold is always one of the most favorite things to rich people, and I should know."

"You forgot the part about not being able to rescue your son, or have you forgotten?"

James looked amused, and said, "No, of course not, how could I? You kept reminding me of it every few hours." He then opened a prepacked lunchbox containing more than twenty sandwiches, and said, "Lunch anyone? I'm starving."

"Shouldn't we be back down there trying to find your son?"

"And why should we do that?"

"Jesus, James, don't you care for your son's wellbeing, even just a little?"

"Of course I do . . . but I'm sure he's quite capable of coming out on his own. Honestly, sometimes I think you don't really know my son at all, do you?"

"How can you be so uncaring, and yet so certain that he will make it out on his own?"

James smiled at her, only the slightest guilt visible. "Because he's already done so."

"Sam's already out of the subterranean waterway?" Aliana asked, too stunned by the news, to be angry.

"Yes, got out a couple days ago."

"What do you mean, 'he got out a couple days ago?' We've been searching for him the past two days, and I was worried sick that he was dead. You knew he was out, but still we went in to get the gold!"

"Yeah, something like that. If it makes you feel better, Sam told me to."

"He told you to. Really?"

"Well, he did say to make sure to keep you safe and hidden, while he was away. So I thought, why not make Rodriguez pay in the process?"

"I thought he was dead, you fucking asshole!" Aliana, for the third time in as many days, since meeting up with James, was ready to kill him. "Hang on. You said while he's away . . . where the hell has he gone?"

"Longjiang, China, of course."

"Oh, of course," she agreed facetiously. "What the hell's he doing there?"

"Elise sent him."

"Why did she send him there?" Aliana paused, as she heard the words in her own ears. "And who's Elise?"

James smiled, speaking slowly as he would to a small child, while explaining something complex. "He's gone to meet a man name Jie Qiang, who might just know exactly where the Mahogany Ship was left."

"And what about the other one . . . the woman you mentioned?"

James stared at her, amusement on his face at her concern at the mention of another woman. "And Elise is a computer whiz that my son hired years ago. She used to consult for the NSA and the FBI until a disagreement on the term 'freedom of information' made her resign—but not without leaving a backdoor into their computer systems, granting her unhindered, and untraceable, access to an immeasurable amount of information."

"Okay . . . so why does Elise think Jie Qiang knows where the Mahogany Ship was left?"

"Because one of his ancestors built it, while the other executed the last man to return from its fatal voyage."

CHAPTER 17

Sam took a commercial flight to China, using a local carrier, and under an alias passport that Elise had prepared for him. He read the email again on the long flight, and recalled the conversation he'd had with the man. Sam had almost deleted the message the first time he saw it, concerned that it might be a ruse orchestrated by Michael Rodriguez or one of his men.

The email had been titled "In the unlikely event you haven't been murdered yet."

He then had Elise look into the email account and run a check on where the message had originated. Determining that it had come from Longjiang, in the northern province of Heilongjiang of the People's Republic of China, she then discovered that the original sender came from a small fishing village, with no known ties to Michael Rodriguez. The only notable history that she could find on the man, was that his entire family had been murdered two years ago.

Elise had suggested he read the letter, and then contact the man through an intermediary.

Sam had read the letter carefully.

Then read it again.

He remembered thinking that, if it was a ruse, it certainly was a very clever one.

By the time he'd finished the conversation, Sam had decided that he must fly directly to meet the man in Longjiang.

Arriving at Qiqihar Sanjiazi Airport, Sam quickly cleared customs, and then took a taxi to a park in Longjiang, overlooking the water of the Long River.

He paid the taxi driver and then, taking out three times the requested fee, asked the driver to wait for him. The driver, staring at the money, assured him he would wait.

Sam walked through the park until he reached two sets of tourist chairs. Sitting down, he examined the large river ahead. Within minutes, another man came and sat next to him.

"The river's very pretty today, isn't it?" Sam said to the stranger.

"It is, but . . . I do not think I would like to go for swim," the man replied, in broken English, confirming that he was the man Sam was looking for.

Sam turned to face the man and said, "Okay, Mr. Jie Qiang. You have my attention; how did you know I was about to be murdered?"

"Because, the man who murdered my family had already gotten what he wanted from you."

"And what was that?"

"Your father's attention," Jie Qiang replied.

"So he thought he could ransom me?"

"No, nothing of the kind. He knew that if you advertised the fact that the Mahogany Ship had been discovered, your father would come there to see it. And your father, Michael knew, was the only man on earth who held the key to finding the real Mahogany Ship."

"But that's crazy. My father doesn't know how to find it. He and I both tried ten years ago, and after many months, accepted that it was nothing more than a fabled story."

"Are you certain?"

"Yes."

"If that's so, where's your father now?"

A cold shiver went down Sam's spine, as he thought about the question. His father had taken an unusual fatherly interest in his safety, while looking into the Mahogany Ship. He even felt loved when he called his father for help, only to discover that the man was already in Bendigo.

Dad, what were you already doing there?

Jie Qiang looked at his face, and said, "So, your father's already come to Australia, as Michael planned."

Sam ignored the question and then asked, "Why would Michael believe my father could help him find the real Mahogany Ship?"

"Not the ship, only her most valuable possession."

"And what made Michael think that my father could help him in his search for it?"

"The fact that your father was in possession of a map that showed him precisely where it was, but he lacked the ability to locate the first identifying symbol on the map."

"And Michael knows where that first symbol is?"

"Yes, Michael paid me a small fortune to receive my map to it."

"How is it that you came to know where the Mahogany Ship met her demise?"

"Because one of my ancestors built it, while the other executed the last man to sail her," Jie Qiang replied.

"Okay, if that's the case, tell me, what was the most valuable thing the Mahogany Ship was carrying?"

"A secret weapon," the man had answered immediately. "A scepter with the ability to destroy anything in its path with intense heat, reflected from the sun."

"So you're not lying. Okay, you have my attention. Why is it that you're now willing to betray Michael?"

"Two years ago I sold him the original map, taken from a man known only as Rat Catcher, a eunuch slave, who was the last person to see the Mahogany Ship, firmly stuck miles inland, in the large landmass that we now know to be Australia. He had returned to China to get reinforcements."

"Did those reinforcements ever come?"

"No, he was executed for crimes against the emperor. Before his death, he left one of my great ancestors with this detailed map of where it lay stranded, along with his journal from the original voyage. Of course, by this stage the Yongle Emperor had passed. His successor, the Hongxi Emperor, had ordered the suspension of Zheng He's maritime expeditions and destruction of the remaining giant Treasure Ships, due to their rising cost and the need to divert soldiers to fight off the constant attacks from the north. With the giant ships no longer making expeditions, it was impossible for anyone to return to this far away land to find the weapon of mythical powers."

"But someone kept the map."

"My ancestors knew the value of the map and left it for each generation in the hope that one day, someone would retrieve the weapon."

"What happened when you sold Rodriguez the map?"

"I returned home from work one day to find my wife and three children all dead in their beds, and a message — 'Followed your map, no sign of the Mahogany Ship or the weapon. I suggest you take better care when providing information in the future.'"

Sam didn't know what to say to comfort the man. "Tell me what you want me to do."

Sam listened to the man's demands, a smile creeping across his face. "Yes, Mr. Jie Qiang, we have a deal."

With that, Mr. Jie Qiang handed over the copy of the map and a journal of one of the most wretched slaves to have ever sailed aboard the Mahogany Ship.

CHAPTER 18

Sam Reilly read and then re-read the poor man's journal more than a dozen times on the long flight back to Australia.

Next to the old Chinese text were a number of pages, typed on A4 paper and stapled together. They were the best translation Jie Qiang could produce.

He flicked through the pages until he reached the earliest entry that seemed to connect to the story in which he was most interested . . .

Mid Atlantic Ocean–March 5, 1442

My name is Rat Catcher, and on this day I stood watch at the top of the giant crow's nest, scanning the horizon for any glimpse of land. At little over four feet, I am by far the smallest man aboard, but my near perfect eyesight has earned me the position on top of the tallest of our ship's eight masts.

Rat Catcher is not my real name, of course.

I have no idea what name my father once gave me. Nor do I know what name my grandfather once gave my own father. The place in which the battle took place, and the cause for which they had fought, were both just as unfamiliar to me. I do not even know what my age was when all of this took place.

What I do know is that my father lost, and as a consequence, I was captured. Too young to be discarded in death, I was castrated, as the custom would deem sensible, so that I may never seed their enemies, and then sold into slavery.

Unable to recall how far I traveled since that day, I can only imagine that it must be some great distance, as my personal features appear so completely different than those who surrounded me in this new life.

I am short and despite an extraordinary appetite, remain skinny, although what weight I have is derived from wiry lean muscle. My eyes are a weak blue color and my skin vulnerably fair compared with those around me, so that it burns every day when I work on the deck.

I've been traded a number of times as my other masters feared that their possession was inherently weak and would shortly die.

By the time I reached a puberty that would never fully come, I was purchased by my current master, who I've since been told only did so because he thought that I could be trained to fetch rats from the tiny spaces within the hold of his ship.

My master immediately named me Rat Catcher.

More than twenty years has passed since that day, and I now know that my master has grown fond of me, and often calls me by it with some affection. I've sailed with my master across nearly all the seas and visited many lands, although in that time I've never seen people who look quite like myself.

As the years progressed, my master discovered that while I was small and physically weak, I was mentally stronger than any he'd ever met. Being small had given me the opportunity of necessity to be quick of hand and to devise the some of the most unique solutions. Together, I've helped my master claim many lands for his own master.

All men have masters-those who believe they don't are lying only to themselves.

By comparison to myself, my master was a giant. Almost seven feet tall I have heard, and he's won many battles and become a master over the sea. Despite all the lands that he had either befriended or conquered, my master's homeland was under a great siege from a foe who had been fighting them since anyone could remember.

There was some fear that if any more warriors left the homeland, then it might fall victim to the invaders.

In fear of losing the sea that he had come to love dearly, my master chose to take his three greatest ships across the largest of the known oceans in the hope that he might discover a power strong enough to beat his enemies completely.

An old seaman's tale spoke of a people who lived on the other side of the vast ocean who held a weapon so powerful that it could strike an entire army down in one blow. Although, how my master heard of such a story was beyond me, given that no one in living memory had ever crossed the ocean and having done so, returned again.

It was for this purpose that my master led just three ships across the ocean, further from my master's homeland than any of his people had ever traveled. They carried gifts to bring friendship to any civilizations he should meet. And many soldiers to enforce it with powerful weapons.

After nearly three months at sea we landed at the inlet of a strange new land.

Sam skimmed the next few entries, which broadly related to replenishing their food supplies, water, and maintenance of the three ships, until he found what he was after.

New Land, West of the Atlantic. May 31, 1442

After nearly a week of sailing north along the foreign shores, I stood on top of the crow's nest and stared at the monstrosity in the distance. It was a pyramid made of solid rock construction, and looked like a fortress that had proven its ability to defend itself for thousands of years.

It was so tall that, despite its base being at the level of the bay, the highest point was even higher than myself, who was perched at the very top of the two-hundred-foot mast.

At the pyramid's crest, I could see a number of men surrounding something that stood at their center and reflected golden rays of sunlight, so powerful that the entire point appeared to glow with gold.

I gave my report to a messenger half way down the mast, who then relayed it on to my master waiting at the bottom for the first report.

My master appeared confident and in his normally commanding presence, despite the pyramid being just as terrifying as he'd described it.

His calmness changed to urgency when he noted the message regarding the golden cylindrical device.

"Hard to starboard! All ships, hard to starboard."

Even at the top of the mast I heard my master bellow the order.

The signal flag was raised and all three ships turned in unison.

Half way through their turn, it happened.

Still aloft in the crow's nest I had the clearest view of the battle.

A flash of lightning struck the ship ahead of me as though the Gods had struck it down. The heat was so powerful that it blew a hole in the front section of the ship the size of a house.

The ship's commander immediately ordered the catapults, which had already been armed prior to rounding the peninsula, to fire. He even managed to get more than twenty off before he realized what was happening.

The hole in the front of his ship was so large that he was swamped within minutes. Before our ship even managed to complete the turn, the other was on its way to the sea beneath. The next shot struck the ship to his rear and this time its commander did not attempt to return fire but instead focused entirely on keeping his ship afloat. It was a futile attempt and within forty seconds the second ship was on its way to the bottom.

Below, I saw that my master had taken as much of an evasive position as could be expected under attack from such superior weaponry.

He rounded the second sinking ship.

I could do nothing but watch as my master made the painful decision to keep going and let the crew of the second ship drown. By the time the second ship was destroyed, the enemies had taken their Godforsaken weapon and aimed it at my master's ship.

It struck no more than a few feet behind our stern.

The water, more than twenty feet of it, turned to steam, but our ship carried on. As we rounded the peninsula again, a second bolt of energy was released.

This time it made contact with the most aft of the masts.

It was disintegrated instantly, the charred remains of its scout falling onto the deck below–and then we were round the peninsula and safe from its violent rays.

I quickly climbed down the mast in time to hear my master give the command to take the ship due east, away from the violent reach of such a catastrophic weapon.

I have watched my master after many battles over the years, but this one seemed different. There had never been one like this, in which more than two thousand men were lost before the battle even started.

But his ship, thankfully, had survived.

"Rat Catcher–this has been a good day!" my master said.

"Yes, it has, Master," I dutifully agreed, although I had no idea what my master was talking about, after watching two thirds of his fleet die within the space of twenty minutes before any of the ships were even within range to return a single attack.

"Do you know what makes today so very special?" my master asked.

"No, master. I do not."

"That weapon we saw is more powerful than any possessed by all of our enemies and friends alike. Of the entire realm wherein we live, I doubt we would find another like it were we to sail for the rest of our lives and well into the next."

"Nor have I, Master," I agreed.

"And that's why, Rat Catcher-we are going to steal it."

Pyramid Fortress June 10, 1442

It had taken hours for my master to explain how we were going to capture such a powerful weapon, but by the time he had finished I knew exactly what must be done. Regardless of the risk, I would happily take the chance with my own life-because my master had asked.

I followed my master and four other men around the ancient path that cut across the peninsula. The jagged path was cut deep into the rocky mountain. My master moved fast along the dangerous ledge.

To the left, where the mountain could be seen high above, a small pocket of dense vegetation appeared unnatural as it struggled to maintain its grip on the rock.

My master smiled as he looked upon it and said, "Ah, here it is."

"Here what is, Master?" I replied.

"What I've been looking for."

My master grinned, mischievously, as though he were playing a game, reached behind the tree, and pulled hard on something. The sound of wheels and pulleys turning could be heard from somewhere inside the mountain, but nothing else happened.

I looked at my master, but said nothing.

No one else in our party was willing to question my master, either.

Then the boulder twenty feet ahead of us slid to the side.

"Welcome gentlemen, to my father's land."

No one spoke, but the revelation of our master's heritage was palpable.

Each man, slowly crouched down and entered the tunnel. It was cramped, and with the exception of myself, they had to remain stooped to stay inside.

The cavern was dark, making it difficult to see where the opening went.

I looked around. There was nothing to suggest that the cavern had been purposely built, or that it had once been someone's home. There was no evidence of any previous human interaction or other animal, for that matter.

Behind me, I heard the enormous boulder start to move again- closing the gap to the outside world.

One of my master's men tried to move quickly to stop it.

"No, let it close," my master ordered.

"But we'll be trapped!"

My master ignored the man's protest, simply holding him firm with his giant left arm. The boulder finished moving, completing blocking our view of the outside world and leaving us all in total darkness.

No one spoke.

I alone, amongst them, felt entirely comfortably with my master's decision. With religious doctrine, I was confident that my master had a grand purpose in life.

As though I was being rewarded for my faith, I heard the sound of more ropes and pulleys moving. A moment later, a secret door at the back of the cavern opened, and a light-filled room came into view, which was large enough that even my master was able to stand comfortably.

"Follow me, gentlemen," my master ordered as he led the way, only having to crouch to get through the small door before being able to stand tall.

The room opened up and became filled with natural light.

"This is called the king's travel vault. There are several built into this track, so that the king can take refuge when required. In doing so, the king can travel light, with only a few royal guardsmen to accompany him."

"And how did you know about the king's vault?" I asked.

"Because he's my father."

"And what are we doing here, Master?" One of my master's other men spoke up.

"Betraying him."

⚓

We waited for the soldiers to come. From above, we had an uninterrupted view of the path below. It was an easy ambush and we slaughtered all eight men by throwing large rocks down upon them, before they had a chance to warn another watch tower.

We stole their armor and quickly donned it.

It was basic, but identified us as part of the civilization.

Only my master stood out amongst us, because he wore a solid gold pendant around his neck with a jade picture of one of the thirteen creator gods on at the center, making him look regal.

Within two days we reached the eastern side of the Great Tower.

The place looked even more enormous and sinister from our low vantage point as we saw it.

There, we waited until night came.

My master arranged for our ship to be rowed towards the harbor in front of the pyramid fortress as soon as the sun left the horizon and the weapon was rendered useless. They were to come in close and carry plenty of lighting to maintain the façade.

We waited until the second watch of the night, and then went forward towards the Great Tower to steal the most valuable weapon the civilization had harbored for more than a thousand years.

Where luck now played its part.

⚓

As I watched from a distance, my master walked with the confidence of a man who knew that royal blood flowed in his veins as he approached the pyramid.

A royal guard noticed him.

"Master, I thought you'd commenced the attack?" The guard looked nervous, as though he was expecting something to be wrong.

"Soon-but we have a new plan. My father has decreed that I should move the weapon to the edge of the mountain, so we can strike our enemy down when they are on the retreat and believe that they are safe having rounded the crest of the mountain."

"A clever plan, master," the guard replied, obsequiously-obviously keen to avoid confrontation.

Together, my master's men carried the weapon down the stairs and along the ancient stone path that led to the edge of the inlet.

With every sound, my ear pricked with fear as though each one might indicate that the ruse had failed, and that my master's family were going to kill him.

But the sound never came.

By the end of the second watch we reached the rowboat, secretly left at the shore by his crew.

Carefully loading the heavy weapon in the center of the boat, we all knew that any accident resulting in the weapon being lost overboard would mean that it could never be retrieved again.

By the fifth stroke of the oars, I thought we had made it.

"Well Rat Catcher, there's a tale to tell your grandchildren-if you were still capable of having them." My master laughed as he said it.

I started to reply, but he didn't hear what I said.

In the distance, his ship was on fire.

⚓

We rowed faster to our ship only to discover that my master's twin brother had attacked the ship. Our crew were strengthened by the return of their master and were able to fight off the assailants, but not before all but one of the masts were destroyed.

Every man on board then fought hard to save the ship from burning. By the morning, we were far from land, and the fire was doused.

The narrow escape was almost mythical.

My master ordered the men to continue rowing past the next two harbors, with the intention of going ashore at the third to make repairs.

After three days, we reached the third harbor, but as we rowed in towards it our waiting enemy threw thousands of stones at us from the high mountainside. Few reached us, but those that did destroyed everything in their path.

If we had been under sail, we could have never turned around in time.

As it was, the rowers were already at their oars and were able to immediately change the direction of the strokes.

For nearly a week, each time the ship came close to the shore it was attacked. My master became increasingly worried that his enemy had a much better means of communicating from each outpost than he had predicted and would soon attack him with their own warships.

It was a risk that my master was not willing to take.

On the fifth day, he ordered his senior commanders to the deck and said, "It is my intention to return to our homeland with the weapon. We have one mast intact and will be able to keep rowing as we cross. Our supplies are less than I would like, but I fear that any attempt to go ashore to replenish them will put us at far too much risk of losing the weapon. Once we are out to sea, their ships will never find us again."

There was a general agreement with our master that they would be able to successfully row across this vast ocean.

And so, with the fatalism of all slaves who served a master, we rowed towards home.

Again, Sam skimmed through the journal until he reached what he was after—the final chapter in the fate of the Mahogany Ship.

Southern Land, August 8, 1442

I watched as the days went by, and my master struggled to maintain our latitude with the strong winds and currents continuously pushing our ship further south. With all but one of our masts destroyed, we struggled to maintain a northern latitude as we headed east. Instead, we were forced past the southern land.

Our supplies were not going to last with the increased effort caused by the constant rowing.

After three months at sea and the death of one third of the crew to malnutrition, my master made the decision that we would have to come ashore in the new land.

We had no identifiable lands from which to take a bearing, but the temperature suggested that we had deviated much further south than our homeland. By this stage it didn't matter. We were going to have to find some fresh water, food, and some means of repairing the decimated masts.

The shore was edged by a rocky cliff, making it impossible to land.

We followed it for three days before finding a place that allowed a ship to anchor. It had a rocky bottom, but the anchor held in the calm weather. Although it would most likely be useless if the swell or wind picked up at all.

A rowboat was dropped, and my master ordered several of his advisers to come ashore with him.

"You'd best come ashore, too, Rat Catcher-I may need your advice."

I beamed at the praise from my master and dutifully took my place, as the smallest man, at the very front of the rowboat.

The enormous shoulder muscles of the slaves swelled while they rowed towards the alien land. Once we reached the shore, the slaves pulled the rowboat up on to the beach and I scurried up onto the beach.

Our weary group followed my master over the large sand dunes and into the land beyond. It was flat and the flora sparse. This would not be the place to fell trees and rebuild our masts. A large river could be seen up ahead, running towards the ocean. Somewhere it would become fresh and drinkable.

Men went ahead to find it.

And my master paced.

After hours, my master stopped and said, "All right men-what do you make of it?"

"Do you mean where we go from here or if we can even provision at this place?" the chief advisor and oldest person in the party asked.

"Where do we go from here?" my master clarified. "We have already spent nearly a week just trying to find an adequate place to make landfall. Our men are weakening, and we have no way of knowing whether or not this will be our best chance."

"My best prediction is that we are almost due south from the homeland. If we could somehow cross this landmass, we would be in a perfect position to reach north towards home." The navigator spoke.

"Then we should row around this land mass," The leading engineer said. "This land offers little with which to repair your ship, master."

"Do you think it will sail much further, given its long list of wounds?" my master asked.

"No."

"Then the decision has been made for us."

"Tell me, master, what that decision is," the lead engineer asked.

"We're going to carry the ship across this body of land," my master ordered.

It was the sort of stubborn solution that my master would come up with. Something that he knew was as entirely unreasonable as it was necessary, its success a certainty in the giant's mind. I knew that I, along with all the men aboard, would happily follow my master in his belief-towards our certain deaths.

⚓

Again I stood at my post on top of the remaining mast.

At two hundred feet, I was in the best position to ensure that the ship wasn't heading directly for a large reef or rock bed. The rowboats had been used to scout the area, but the eagle's nest offered the best vantage point. From there I could immediately see any changes in the water color and by now I was well accustomed to determining what those changes meant.

On my master's orders the men rowed the ship at full speed towards the sandy beach with the fatality of men who served their master at all cost. I watched as the color turned from a dark blue to a light green, and then finally the sand could be seen below the keel.

There was a loud crunch as the flat bottom of our wooden ship came into contact with sand, followed by a series of vibrations that resonated throughout the ship, causing the eagle's nest to sway ever so slightly.

For a moment I was worried it was going to tear the hull in two.

Then the bow of our gigantic ship reached the sandy beach.

Riding its own wave-which must have been twenty feet high at least, it continued to move high up the first of the shallow sand dunes as if there had been nothing in our way. Her momentum carried her forward like the monster she was.

We passed all four sand dunes as though they weren't even there.

The ship finally came to rest more than a hundred feet along the new, flat, earthy land. So much water had come with us that our massive ship now appeared to be resting in a small lake of its own creation, several feet deep and as much as a mile wide.

⚓

My master seemed invigorated by the progress we were making.

He stood on the highest hill in the distance and examined his ship. It had been a week, and still it rested in a small lake. It appeared bigger, if that was even possible, out of the water.

Men were working in all directions. Tasks had been set and teams had been formed to achieve specific purposes. My master confided in me that they were already looking much better for their efforts. Men needed tasks. Idleness often bred poor health. So did a lack of nutrients, but that too was in the process of being rectified.

A great foraging party had been sent for miles in all directions to return with provisions. Strange new animals had been found and slaughtered. A great variety of berries had been located and those rich in nutrients were identified, compared with those that were lethal. The men followed their orders and tested the new foods until the ship's master doctor had a long list of edible, difficult, and lethal plants and animals.

The engineer had used more than two hundred men to make changes to the ship. Large parts of the rigging, oars and weaponry were cannibalized in order to build a system by which the monstrous ship could be carried by an army of loyal men.

Today, the master engineer had ordered a party of three hundred men to remove the remaining water from the lake so that he could make the final adjustments to the base of the ship.

It reassured my master to watch the men work with such loyal efficiency as they removed the water by hand held bucket.

By the end of the day, the senior engineer approached my master.

"We are ready master."

"Excellent. We leave at once."

⚓

It had been three weeks since we had first started carrying the Godforsaken ship. The land was terribly dry and unforgiving. I was starting to question the wisdom of my master's decision to naively cross an alien land in the hope that it was a narrow body of land with a northern ocean nearby.

But still we pressed on through both day and night with carrying teams rotating constantly. We numbered fifteen hundred men, and it required nearly a thousand at any one time to lift the ship. Teams of ten on each carrying oar would rotate further down every half an hour until they reached the end of the ship and were thus allowed a break.

In doing so, each man would obtain a four-hour break throughout a twenty four hour period.

By the end of the third day and the death of ten men who literally pushed their bodies to death, my master realized that carrying the ship through the night was going to be impossible.

The days continued on, and we traveled a little less each day.

By the end of the second week we no longer had enough healthy men to rotate the carrying shifts through the day. For a while the men succeeded in maintaining the ship's movement with a twenty-minute break in the middle of the day. Then, their ability to carry it became less, and they were no longer able to carry the ship throughout the entire daylight hours.

By the third week, my master accepted that the ship could only realistically be moved for four hours each day. The rest of the time the men would be required to gather provisions and prepare the land in front of them, which often required the felling of many trees to allow the movement of the great ship.

As we reached the start of the fifth week, our numbers had dwindled to the point that the entire ship could only be moved every other day and even then for only a matter of hours.

With my master's encouragement, the men were able to maintain this effort until the eighth week when they were no longer able to move the ship more than twenty or so feet in the day.

"We'll rest here for a week if we have to," my master said. "You have all honored me with your effort, but to go on further at this pace would be to ask for failure. We shall rebuild our health and then continue. Surely, the sea must be close. I can smell the salt in the air."

I have an unusually sensitive nose, and I was certain my master was merely encouraging the men.

The men rested for an entire week and then commenced again.

But the rest time hadn't improved their condition.

If anything, it had made things worse. Prior to the break, men had continued to work with injuries. Now, those injuries had been allowed to fester.

Over the course of the next week, more people died and many more became no longer capable of carrying heavy weights.

Again, my master ordered a meeting with his most trusted advisers and again, he requested my attendance-although for what purpose, I did not know. I certainly didn't have any expertise in the area to offer.

This time, he did not ask for our opinion on how to solve the problem, but instead demanded each person to identify equipment and materials on board the ship that could be discarded.

It then took another week to decide on which provisions to discard and which equipment could be done without.

This time our efforts appeared to have been worthwhile, and the ship continued to move in a northern direction for a few hours each day. But within a few days we were back to removing more items from the ship's complement.

It was on our ill-fated crew's eighty-ninth day that, despite my master's encouragement and his orders, the ship was no longer capable of being moved.

It sunk into the mud-soaked land.

Each day, she seemed to rest lower, her new master gaining an unmovable strangle hold.

This time, the Mahogany Ship had found her final resting place.

⚓

I was prepared to die so that my master may succeed, but had no intention of leaving my master to ruin.

Over the next three weeks it became overly apparent to everyone involved that the new land, rich in beauty as it was sparse and desolate, had no means of providing for the remaining men. Working parties had been sent out in all directions to fend for themselves.

As each leader returned, only one thing was certain.

The crew of the Mahogany Ship must abandon her and disperse if anyone was to survive. And survive we must, because we had discovered the most powerful weapon the world had ever known. If only we could reach our homeland.

"The master wants to speak with you," said the chief navigator.

"Just me?" I asked.

"Just you."

"Where is he?"

"In his master cabin-where else?" The navigator shook his head disloyally. "He spends hours each day inside there, just looking at it-you know? I think it's driven him quite mad. Power does that, you know, and we've all witnessed just how much power that thing yields."

Ordinarily I would have reprimanded even someone as senior as the chief navigator for attacking my master. But I could see what was happening and knew that now was not the time to overplay my master's authority. I could feel that there would be mutiny before all persons succumbed to starvation.

"I'll go to him immediately."

I climbed the steps up and into the master cabin at the aft of the grand ship. It was larger than the average house back home and fit for a king. In this case, it housed my master, a would-be king, and wielder of the most powerful weapon mankind had ever built.

"Rat Catcher-have you come alone?" my master asked immediately.

"Yes, Master."

"Good. Very good." In the middle of the room stood the magnificent weapon, its sparkling gems glistening in the dim light of a candle. My master spoke, but at no time did his eyes look away from the evil weapon that had driven us to our current state. "Five weeks ago, I believe every single man aboard this ship would have happily given their lives if I asked them to. But as you know, a lot has changed in that time. Hungry men will do many things they never would have previously dreamed of if they are hungry enough."

"Master . . ."

"Wait . . . I'm not finished. I cannot maintain command of the Mahogany Ship for much longer, and I cannot risk losing my master's great weapon. So I will tell you what must be done."

"You will always be my master!" I protested.

"Of course I will. You always were a fool, and a foolish man alone dies serving a master who cannot provide for him basic sustenance." My maser's hand almost touched the precious stone, but then withdrew it as though it were poison.

"What would you have me do, Master?"

"I need to disband my crew. Even fools must understand that this new land, sparsely inhabited, is incapable of providing for the men in such close proximity. I have broken my crew into eight groups, each under a different leader's command. I will send them in all directions in search of food and help. I will remain here to guard the weapon–I cannot even imagine the consequence of its power falling into the hands of our master's enemies."

"And for me?"

"I have a different plan."

Homeward Bound, September 1, 1442.

In the early hours of the next morning, well before the sun had risen, I left with another seven of my master's most trusted men. We were on our way back to the southern land where we had arrived so long ago.

We moved quickly, hindered only by meagre provisions and no personal belongings, with the exception of one scroll on which I was to continue this journal in the hope of one day retracing our steps.

At the end of the first day, I stopped and made some notes in this very book. It is the one that my master gave me so that I could record our journey and so one day return to retrieve the weapon for the homeland.

I had pleaded with my master to let me stay by his side, but in the end he ordered me. And so I now obey his wishes.

"Should we try and bring the weapon back with us?" I had asked.

"No, you won't be able to protect it," my master had responded. "The rowboat may sink, and if it does then the weapon will be lost forever. Worse still, you may be captured by any one of my master's enemies. If that were to happen and the weapon lost, I would be the one responsible for the collapse of my master's reign."

"Then, should we carry it closer to the shore where we first landed?"

"No, then someone else may come across it. Leave the weapon here, and I will guard it so long as I'm alive." My master had then handed me the scroll and said, "Take this. I have made the first entry in it-our position in relation to those mountains in the north, the river to the south, and the desert to the west."

I had taken the book and held it as if it were the most valuable possession I'd ever had.

"Keep your entries clear, and make them often so that you alone may one day return with enough men to fetch the weapon. Don't fail me in this, Rat Catcher."

My master had tears in his eyes as he spoke. As do I, now that I make my own entries in this journal.

The days went by and we continued to move quickly. I made entries in my journal often, until we reached the shore where our wooden rowboat had been deserted.

During that time, the weather had changed considerably for the colder.

"The seasons are changing-we must find a way north before we freeze here," I told my men, of whom I was now master.

"Of course, Master. The rowboat will be ready within the hour."

"Good-we must complete our journey so that we can return in time to save our master."

All eight of us then loaded the rowboat and started our long journey home.

The sea was rough and demanded all the strength and intellect we could muster not to capsize. After three days of continuous rowing we reached the southern tip of the land. A number of strange currents ran in both directions and it took us a further three days to finally round the point and head north.

On the first beach that appeared accessible I gave the order to land so that we were able to find fresh water and resupply.

Our party found that we were able to row in a northern direction almost continuously for months on end. Regularly beaching the rowboat for a day or two-just enough time to find fresh water and scavenge for food-sustained us.

We never stayed very long on any of the beaches, fear telling us that the dark colored locals may be violent. More often than not, the native people appeared more frightened than anything else and kept their distance. Even so, I had no intention of remaining long enough for a physical confrontation. The eight of us would make a poor army and would be vulnerable on land.

After three months, we reached the top of the massive landmass and were once again able to head west where surely our homeland must be.

We navigated by the stars as best we could, but none of us could recognize much of what we saw. I alone knew that we must travel further north, but had no way of knowing just how far that was. We rowed hard, driven by the fanatical desire not to betray our master's trust.

Almost three years later, I and the other seven men aboard entered the grand harbor which we had once called home, now so long ago.

Longjiang, January 1446

I stepped off the rowboat at the busy port I once called home.

I felt no fear.

My boat was only one of over a hundred inside the harbor, and no one looking at us could have imagined where we had come from.

Except that the front of the boat was still ordained with the name of my master's ship.

Barloc Wikea.

"You there-who is in charge?" It was one of the harbor guards.

"I am," I replied.

"And who are you?"

"I do not know what my father named me, but my master has always called me Rat Catcher."

"Then who is your master and where is he now?" The man was being intentionally rude.

"My master is Barloc . . ."

The man didn't let me finish.

"And where has Barloc gone? He left with three of our greatest ships-there is an order to have him executed upon his return for treason."

"Treason!" I complained. "He was the emperor's most loyal servant."

"Then where is he?"

"His ship was damaged in a far off land and he has remained to guard its most awesome treasure, which he has captured in the name of the emperor."

The man started to laugh.

"And you expect me to believe this!"

I was about to run, but someone had already gripped my wrists and bound them with rope.

All eight of us were taken to a prison until our fate could be decided.

Three days later a man entered the prison and advised us that we were all to be executed the following morning for treason.

"But we are loyal servants of the emperor. Please, we come bearing news of Barloc's great achievements and to guide a ship to retrieve the greatest of treasures," I pleaded.

"You have been away a long time, haven't you?"

Unable to decide what was expected, I remained silent.

"We were losing so many men to battles upon distant shores that we were no longer able to keep our enemies from attacking our cities. The emperor decreed that his navy may no longer leave the harbor."

"No, but it must. Within the treasure that my master has claimed for the emperor, lies a weapon so powerful that it will yield unstoppable strength to its owner. I have seen it with my own eyes destroy an entire ship with seconds."

"That is not my concern. I am here to inform you that tomorrow morning you will be executed."

The man was obdurate.

That night I called for a guard. The man appeared young, maybe less than sixteen years old and of all the sentries I'd seen, this one appeared most ill at ease around the prisoners.

I relayed the story of our adventure to the young man. Where we had been, and what we had seen-and how my master had stayed with the stricken ship to protect the treasure so that the emperor could rule for eternity.

The boy tried his best to explain that he couldn't help us escape, even if he had wanted to.

He has gone now, but when he returns in a few hours, I will shove these writings into his hand and make him promise to do what I could not, and return for my master.

I only hope that these words will one day lead you to find my master and return the weapon to the emperor.

Sincerely, Rat Catcher.

CHAPTER 19

The large and cumbersome Chinook had been replaced by the much smaller and agile Bell UH-1Y Venom, AKA, Super Huey. With Tom at the controls, Sam sat comfortably as the craft flew over the Victorian town of Castlemaine and on towards Echuca, where Aliana and his father were waiting for them. They were going to follow Rat Catcher's original map, from the Southern Ocean all the way back to where the Mahogany Ship had been finally destroyed.

Sam found them sitting by an old, beat up Holden Utility, parked on the edge of town.

"What took you so long?" his father asked.

Sam ignored the question and walked up to Aliana. "I'm sorry to leave you with my dad, but I couldn't risk Rodriguez finding out I'd escaped."

For a moment, he thought she might slap him, and even braced himself for the pain.

And then she wrapped her long, slender arms around his neck, and kissed him. "If you ever do that to me again, don't expect to see me here when you return."

"I won't, I promise."

James loaded the equipment into the helicopter and the team of four carried on towards the Barmah National Park along the Victorian border.

From the air, Sam remembered the story Jie Qiang told of Barloc's men having attempted to carry the massive ship all the way from the southern coast, in an attempt to cross the enormous land mass and gain latitude. He tried to picture the monstrous ship being dragged over the crest of the hills, and for a moment, pictured creeks and troughs in the mountains as though they were possibly caused by the movement of the ship.

"Let's have a look at this map," his father said. "You spent nearly six months in Longjiang, trying to find a lead about this map, and now, you're telling me one of our enemies found it first?"

"Yes, I know. Jie Qiang told me that he'd heard you talking to someone from his town. It was only then that he realized just how valuable this map really was."

"Right, well I hope you didn't pay him too much for it. After all, it's practically useless, without this map, too," James said as he pulled out his great, great, Grandmother Rose's map.

"Let's hope they're both right."

Tom smiled as his eyes skimmed over the map. "I just can't believe there isn't a supermarket, or shopping mall, built over the top of it."

They flew over a number of rivers, including the great Murray-Darling, which Sam imagined had moved its banks many times in the centuries that had passed since the Mahogany Ship was carried through this area.

Still he followed the map, until no more markers were left.

And there, below them, rested the depressed marks of what could only have once been the most extraordinarily large ship of ancient times. No wood remained, and grass and trees had grown where the ship once rested, but from the air, there was still no mistaking this was the final resting place of the Mahogany Ship.

Michael Rodriguez looked at the drawing his great ancestors had made of the Ark of Light, all those millennia ago. It brought back memories of the first time his father told him of his true purpose in life.

That his family had been chosen, thousands of years ago, to look after a sacred artefact that held the key to unlock all of mankind's unimaginable powers. He still recalled the shame that he felt as his father explained that his family, sworn to protect the scepter, had lost it nearly a six years ago. Followed by the pride to know that he would one day discover it again.

But of course, he had no intention of protecting it. A device that offered such power would surely be a waste to keep buried. No, soon it would be his, and with it, he would introduce a new system of power on earth.

Sam had done just as he wanted, and soon, his father would lead him straight to it.

"Okay, dad, do you want to read out that map of yours for me?" Sam asked, staring at the desolate land around them and wondering how such a monumental historical artefact could disappear into the sands of time, in such a place.

"No need, I've read it enough to know it verbatim."

"All right then, let's hear it."

"We need to fly exactly 22 miles due north of the northern tip of the bow of the Mahogany Ship," James said. "And, before you ask, we're going to need this to be exact, so let's work out where the different tips of the ship are."

"Okay, I think it's there," Sam said, pointing to the ground to the right of them.

Aliana leaned over, kissing him on his cheek, and said, "Good guess darling, but I think you're wrong. Zheng He's treasure ships had a two-tiered bow, meaning that the deep imprints that we can see now are the main keel, whereas the final southern tip would be another fifty feet back."

"She's right son. Didn't you study archeology or something at some stage as a minor?"

"Egyptology, to be exact—never ancient China."

Tom banked to the left to make a large circle before starting the trip from precisely fifty feet back from where Sam had suggested the northern tip of the ship had once been.

"Everyone happy?" Tom said.

There was a general murmur of agreement, before they continued on along the treasure hunt.

Aliana picked up and then looked at the old map. "Hey James, what makes you think any of these markers on this map are still there?"

"Because old Jack Robertson may have been a murdering bastard, but as a crooked highwayman he'd been used to burying treasure for years. If anyone knew how to make a map that couldn't be tainted by time, it was old Jack. Just look at this—all we have to do is find the tip of the highest point inside these three points and then walk north 150 feet. Easy."

After the 22-mile flight, Tom said, "Now where?"

Sam's father then pulled out the map that he said he'd memorized and looked at the landscape. "Just hover there for a minute, would you?"

"You're the boss, James."

Almost immediately, he put the map down and said, "Okay, take us down, over there."

Landing on the top of the mountain, Sam used the helicopter's radar to determine if there was another mountain within fifty miles higher than the one they were on — and there wasn't. "Well dad, I guess you have a bit more luck this time."

Together, the four members of the team counted 150 feet, and then stopped.

The land was dry, with a few hardened native shrubs, the only plants to be seen.

James looked around and happily said, "This is it. Here's the spot."

"That's great. Where's the Ark of Light?" Aliana asked.

"Below us . . . well, actually, it's somewhere down a river that's below us."

Sam jumped up and down a couple times and said, "The soil appears pretty sturdy to me. Did you have a plan of getting to the river below?"

"Yeah. Tom, do you mind running back to the helicopter and grabbing that box I brought, while I dig a hole?"

Tom nodded his head and then ran back to the helicopter, returning a few minutes later with the box.

"What did you bring, dad?"

"Dynamite. I'm not sure how old it is. I found it on the old homestead I was staying at, and thought it might come in handy."

"Shit, you could have killed us. Do you have any idea how unstable that stuff is, particular after a number of years, rotting away?"

James laughed, "I'm only kidding. It's just ANFO, ammonium nitrate/fuel oil, the more contemporary, and cheaper, explosive commonly used in mainstay mining and just a little more stable."

Sam, by this stage, had dug nearly three feet deep in the soft soil, but each time he tried to dig further, more surrounding sand seemed to fill the hole.

"You want to keep digging until you reach that river, or shall I use the ANFO and speed the process up a little?"

"Be my guest," Sam said, stepping away from the hole.

Sam watched as his father laid the ANFO and set the charge cable with surprising dexterity, making him wonder just how many times his father had done this before.

"All right, everyone back . . . and I mean a long way back."

Five minutes later, James pulled the detonating switch, and the ground in the distance disappeared. Slowly, the small party of four, walked up to where the hole had been. What remained was a limestone cavern large enough to drive a truck through. And at the bottom, a small creek flowed gently, into the unknown.

Rodriguez drove his six-wheeler at a pace that would have made the German engineers at Mercedes proud. He knew where they were headed, but still hadn't taken into account that they'd use a damn helicopter, making them a lot faster.

Behind him, Frank and Byron struggled to keep up in their own six-wheelers, each armed with an AK 47, loaded and ready to go.

Up ahead, and to the left of them, a giant plume of black smoke reached for the sky, followed by a loud boom, four or five seconds afterwards.

"Shit, they've already reached it!" Rodriguez said out loud, as he swung the wheel and headed towards the smoke. His foot to the floor, he challenged every inch of the million dollar Mercedes's engineering price tag.

Sam reached for the fourth dive tank from the back of the helicopter, ready to follow the stream down as a team of four.

Aliana put her hand on it, effectively stopping him from removing the tank. "No way. I'm not following you or any of your other crazy people down through another one of those stupid subterranean rivers. I've been there, done that—not again."

"Really? I thought you'd had fun." Sam grinned. "That's all right, but I think you're underestimating the significance of the Ark of Light!"

"I doubt it. I've heard little of anything else from your father since you left. Says it has the ability to provide him with unlimited power . . . I thought that's what he already has?"

The two started walking towards the opening where the subterranean river flowed. Sam laughed. "Yes, that sounds like my father, but this could be the greatest historical artefact ever found. It could bring peace to the world, and in the wrong hands, destroy it."

"I hate to be the pessimist, but in the hands of mankind, I fear it's more likely to do the latter. So what, exactly, is it supposed to do?"

As they approached the cave, Sam saw that his father, already inside it, had started to run out a long cable, and smiled at Aliana, as though she, like a naive child, would never understand the importance of gold and power.

"This scepter," Sam continued, "when placed on top of the Pyramid of Giza at the midday of winter solstice in the year 2020, will point to the final vault of the ultimate artefact — the God's Relic, an ancient requiem of all human knowledge, from the first cycle."

"What do you mean by first cycle?" Aliana asked.

James smiled as he overheard the conversation. Sam recognized it as his 'I'm about to tell you something that will blow your mind type smile' and then replied, "The generation of humans before present day civilization occurred."

Aliana turned her head slightly as she thought about what he'd said. "We weren't the first?"

"Not even the second, I'm afraid. The human race only ever seems to evolve to a certain state, before we inevitably wipe ourselves out. Some civilizations get further than the next, but somehow we always seem to mess it up. It's in our nature," James said.

"And where do we fit into this? Are we the furthest along the stream of evolution?"

James thought about the question for a moment and then replied, "No. And we're unlikely to beat some of the more successful civilizations."

Aliana stared at him. Her expression told them she was considering if there could really be any truth to any of it.

"Legend has it that this scepter holds the key to a vault, which contains all human knowledge, spanning all the cycles of civilizations gone by," Sam said.

"How does the information get there?"

"No one knows. Some people have hypothesized that earth has a caretaker . . . like God, who keeps an eye on things, and stores all the information that man accumulates until a cycle finally becomes so intelligent as to break the code."

"What code?" she asked.

"The ability to not destroy yourself. Something that so far, all civilizations before us have failed to do."

"That's ridiculous. It's in the same realm as a child being told that Santa Claus delivers presents to children all over the world in a single night!"

Grinning mischievously, Sam said, "Then again, it might just have been a longstanding fable, like the Mahogany Ship, that means nothing . . ."

Aliana clearly didn't believe a word his father had said. She replied, "Well this sounds very exciting, but if it's all the same to you, I think I'll just wait here until you retrieve it."

"Very good," James said, then throwing his dive gear over his shoulders, impatiently said, "We'll see you soon."

Sam kissed her and said, "I won't be long."

Tom then looked at him, and said, "Actually, I'm going to leave this one to you and your father. I'm going back for the truck you stole earlier. Based on the weight predictions that James has given me, there's no way I'll get the Super Huey off the ground with that thing on board."

"You don't want to dive now, and go back for it afterwards?"

"No, it's going to take a couple hours to get back with it, and I don't want to be flying once it's dark. Let's not forget that Rodriguez and his men are still searching for it, too."

"Good point." Sam said, unconcerned. "While you're there, you might want to load the wooden crate from the Chinook, too."

"Okay, will do."

Sam picked up his netted duffle bag, and then slid into the water. Surface swimming to the end of the tunnel, he then disappeared below the surface.

Ahead of him, Sam found his father dragging the cable over his shoulder.

He caught up quickly and switched on his high powered, rock penetrating sonar so he could see the images of any heavy metals below.

The two swam on.

Like its surface siblings, the subterranean river meandered side to side as it searched for the easiest means of travelling towards the ocean hundreds of miles away.

By the third corner, nothing was visible below with his naked eyes, but the sonar monitor displayed something.

It was the outline of a staff, about six feet long. And next to it, a sheet of metal, no larger than a piece of A4 writing paper.

"I think we found it, Dad."

James looked at the monitor.

"Either that, or we found its twin."

The two swam another twenty feet below the water, where the Ark of Light lay entirely buried by two centuries of river silt.

CHAPTER 20

Sam withdrew four inflatable bags from his duffle bag and carefully attached them to the Ark of Light, still mostly buried.

His father, impatient as always, tried vainly to lift the scepter by hand so that he could better examine it. But in the soft river bed, his feet were unable to obtain enough perch to lift it.

Sam slowly filled each bag with the air from his dive regulator. "We've waited a lifetime to see this, Dad. Surely it won't kill you to wait until we get it back to the cave before we examine it."

"I suppose you're right," James said; his hand stabilizing the now buoyant Ark of Light, and attaching the cable to the end of it.

Sam studied the monitor of his sonar again to make certain he hadn't missed anything. "What about this?"

His dad looked over his shoulder, and said, "Looks like a really old piece of paper, to me. What do you think, the instructions for the weapon?"

"I doubt it. But if Jack Robertson thought it was important enough to go to the trouble of taking it with him, there must be something to it."

"You're right, go see if you can find it below all that silt, and I'll start bringing this to the surface."

Sam fished his hands through the soft silt until he found what he was looking for. It was made of brass, and despite the filth of being submerged for so many years, Sam could clearly see the writings painstakingly chiseled into it.

And they were written in the ancient text of the Master Builders.

He couldn't make out every word. He would need Billie's help for that, but he could make out enough of them to understand the purpose of the message.

> THE ARK OF LIGHT MUST BE RETURNED TO ITS RIGHTFUL PLACE, ON TOP OF THE GREAT PYRAMID OF GIZA, BY MIDDAY OF . . . WINTER . . . S. . . . IN THE YEAR 2020 BEFORE THE END OF THIS CYCLE. TO BE ACTIVATED, IT MUST BE JOINED WITH ITS OTHER SIBLINGS, OR IT WILL NOT WORK.

It then listed four locations.

The first three he couldn't quite make out, but the last one, he'd certainly heard of.

ATLANTIS.

Sam put the brass tablet in his duffle bag and quickly swam to catch up with his father.

By the time he reached the cave, his father was already trying to drag the heavy Ark of Light on to the beach of the cave.

Sam helped him lift it onto the beach, and then explained to his father what the note Barloc had left, said.

"Well, that's just great, isn't it?" James stood up, ready to leave the cave. "It's taken me sixty eight years to locate this device, only to discover that it needs to be armed with four other relics before it will show me the way — and the only one we've even heard of has been thought to be nothing more than a legend by the world's best archeologists."

"All right dad, let's get this thing up top, and see what Aliana's doing. Then we can work out what our next move is."

It took all their strength to drag it to the top of the cave and out into the open.

At the edge of the tree line, Aliana appeared still as a rock.

"Aliana," Sam called out. "We did it!"

It was then that she turned around and mouthed something to him. He couldn't quite see what she was trying to say, until it was too late, but he could see the sickening expression on her face.

"Oh shit!" James said, realization hitting him faster, and throwing himself on Sam.

A moment later, the powerful staccato of the UZIs raked the ground they were standing on.

The two fell, head first, down the cave.

Sam, rolled as he landed and quickly looked around the room to see how he could arm himself. He surprised by the speed his father had reacted.

"You all right, son?"

"Fine, but they've got Aliana!"

"We'll get her back," James reassured him.

They heard the sound of the machine gun raking the entrance of the cave, and the two quickly dived into the water.

Above, they heard the sound of someone entering the cave and shooting over the top of the water. Bullets, slowed by the drag of water, fell harmlessly above them.

After a couple minutes, Sam heard a loud bang, as a grenade destroyed the roof of the cave, leaving them in complete darkness.

Aliana watched in horror as the man she loved was buried alive for the second time in a week. And she wondered if he could possibly be lucky enough to survive it twice. That was, if the blast hadn't killed him already. Her thoughts then turned to the man who'd betrayed him, Michael Rodriguez. Her anger rose as she considered the sinister, power hungry man, behind the friendly façade.

"Aliana, how lovely it is to see you again." She recognized the voice instantly.

"Rodriguez. You surprise me. I thought a man of your caliber wouldn't stoop to get your hands dirty? When I saw your lackeys, I guessed, they were under your orders, but hadn't expected to see you here, too."

Michael dipped his hat, and said, "Your words compliment me, greatly. I've always prided myself on being willing to get involved in every aspect of my work—even when that involves, getting them dirty, as you say. Besides, as a mining magnate, it's my duty to return an area of destruction to its normal view after it has been mined. My men just removed that ugly eyesore from the ground, where a hole once was."

"You can call it what you will—you just murdered Sam Reilly and his father. Although you may not have considered it, I'm sure that sort of thing comes with some serious repercussions."

"It is, as you say, frowned upon in civilized society to kill a billionaire and his brat son, but hey, out here, they're just a couple of guys in the middle of the woods, am I right?" Rodriguez laughed, as though he were having a casual conversation with a neighbor. "If you must know. I never had any intention to murder Sam. He's a bright man. I would have gladly let him continue to think he'd discovered the Mahogany Ship, while his old man and I conducted our business. But the kid just couldn't let it go, could he? He was too smart, and had to figure it all out. Heck, I still can't work out how he escaped last time."

Aliana looked at Rodriguez — he was talking to himself more than her — and wondered if she could kill him before either of his two goons with AK 47s noticed.

But how?

"Have you said your good byes to your dear Sam Reilly?"

"No, his father taught me that Sam's not an easy man to get rid of. I think you'll find that they're both far more resilient than you give them credit for."

"Confidence. I like to see that in a woman!" Rodriguez said. "Good for you. I wonder how long it will last, after I keep you to see firsthand the power revealed by the Ark of Light. After all, I'm soon to bring a new global order. Like it or not, you may as well start obeying me now."

It was Aliana's turn to laugh. "New global order. I thought you were a common thief and murderer, but I see that you're just crazy."

"Laugh now, but you may as well accept your boyfriend's dead, and I'm about to change the course of history." Rodriguez, seeing that his story wasn't entertaining anyone but himself, turned to his men, and said, "Stay here, cover it properly, make sure no one's ever going to mistake it for the entrance to something. I want it buried properly. And then I'll be waiting for you with the plane in Sydney."

"Understood, boss."

Rodriguez then took out a large handgun and pointed it at

Aliana. If she'd known anything about weapons, she'd have known that it was a Smith and Wesson .500 Magnum, the most powerful production handgun in existence. Recently advertised as the weapon of choice as, "A Hunting Handgun for any Game Animal," due to its ability to take down an elephant at a reasonable distance.

Aliana didn't need to know that, though. She saw Rodriguez's cheery face and knew that he meant business. "Now, we can do this my way, or the hard way. Frankly, I don't mind my women difficult. They all come around, soon enough, even the rich ones, with enough incentive."

Aliana didn't want to give him any chance to physically display his power over her. She stepped up into the large Mercedes 6x6. Rodriguez followed after her and, taking out a pair of cable ties, locked her wrists together.

"Nothing personal, dear, but I can't have you causing me trouble while I'm driving. You understand, it's just not safe."

She said nothing, and Rodriguez started back the way he came.

Aliana took one last look at the buried land behind her, where the man she loved had disappeared.

CHAPTER 21

Tom drove down the dry, corrugated, dirt road into Barmah National Park. It had taken him slightly longer than he'd expected, but at least he wouldn't be an obvious target since leaving the Super Huey in Echuca. Driving along the edge of the Murray-Darling River, Tom pulled off the beaten road, and into the rough scrub, towards where he'd left his friends. On the horizon, two large dust clouds reached for the sky. They were most likely four wheel drives, heading off to go hunting in the kangaroo filled dusk.

He followed his GPS until it assured him he was at the right spot.

There was nothing around. Admittedly, there was very little around when he'd left, but now he couldn't see any remnants of the hole that James had created when he blew an entrance to the river below.

He parked the old Holden Utility about twenty feet from where he was certain the hole had been when he left, and then got out of the car. It was approaching dusk, and the sullen color of the sky played tricks on people.

Tom checked his hand-held GPS again, and confirmed he was in the right spot. He then stepped over the ground and noticed that the sand was soft, as though recently disturbed.

Up ahead, he noticed the deep four-wheel drive tracks in the sand.

He then recalled the dust clouds on the horizon as he drove in — *Rodriguez's men!*

There wasn't much time.

Tom grabbed a shovel and started digging.

He'd dug no more than a foot before hitting something solid, with a loud clank. Steel — someone had laid a steel frame over the remains of the hole and then backfilled it with sand to make it look like nothing had ever happened.

If they'd gone to the lengths to do so, Tom had a fair idea why.

He ran back to the Utility, and ran a twenty-foot chain from his tow bar to the steel covering, running a hook through an attachment point.

Then ran back to his vehicle and floored its old, and powerful, V8 engine.

His tires slipped in the soft soil, and then caught, and the entire steel plate, along with sand on top, pulled away.

Tom pulled over and ran back.

Where Sam and James were clawing their way back up the hole in the ground.

James grinned through the dirt on his grubby face, and said, "What took you so long, Tom? We've got work to do."

Sam jumped into the driver's side of the car. Not waiting to fill Tom in with what had happened, he said, "They've got a twenty-minute head start on us, and they've got Aliana."

"Shuffle over son, I'll drive," James said, pushing his way in front of the steering wheel, forcing Sam to slide further down the old bench seat.

"Whatever . . . let's just go," Sam replied, urgently.

James had his foot down, testing just how fast the old muscle car could go. In the wide-open, desolate land, the poor handling and poor cornering didn't matter. The powerful V8 was in its prime, and the car quickly sped up to 65 miles per hour and on to 80.

They were following the only other tracks in the otherwise barren land.

By the time it was dark outside, they could see the tail lights of a car up ahead. The car seemed to be travelling at a normal speed, probably comforted in the knowledge that they had already won the battle.

"Say, Sam, do you have a plan what we're going to do when we catch up to these guys, or do you just want to wing it?"

"I'm all for winging it. Dad, if you can get closer, then start to overtake the car, and then swerve into its rear left axle, we might just send that top-heavy truck onto its roof. Then, the three of us jump out and kill whoever's driving, while he's still confused about what happened — and save the girl." Sam looked at his father who said nothing, but looked like he'd raised an idiot. "What, you have a better idea? We didn't bring any weapons, and it's not like we've time to go back and get them."

"As a matter of fact, son. I do." James then looked at Tom and asked, "Did you leave that wooden box in the back of the cargo tray?"

"Yeah, why?"

"See if the two of you can climb back there and open it."

"What's in it?" Sam asked.

245

"Open it up, I'm sure you'll know what to do with them."

Sam began following Tom, who had climbed out through the passenger window, over the roof and into the cargo tray behind. When he was half way out, the left front tire struck something, hard—sending the car violently swerving towards the left, where it fishtailed for a hundred or so feet and then kept going.

His hand clutching onto the roof like a vice, he held on long enough for the centrifugal force to stop, and then he was flung back inside as James regained control.

"Next time, a little warning would be nice."

"See what I can do, but no promises, son."

Sam quickly climbed into the back of the utility, where he found Tom grinning like a kid who'd just discovered his father's firecrackers.

"What is it, Tom?"

"Well, in a country with severe restrictions on firearms, your father managed to bring these with him—just in case," Tom said, opening the wooden box.

"Holy shit!

Inside were two M9 bazookas, an M60 machine gun, and a large sawn-off shotgun.

"What does Dad want us to do, blow Aliana up?" Sam then tapped on the back window and said, "Hey, did you bring anything here that we can actually use?"

"Hey, I thought you two were a couple of old boy scouts—I brought the hardware, you decide what you want to do with it."

"All right, all right . . . just get us a little closer, and then hold us steady."

Sam then picked up the M9.

"Are you kidding me? That thing has an armor piercing head, designed to take out a tank. I thought you liked this girl?"

"Don't worry, I have no intention of hitting their vehicle. Now load me."

Behind him, Tom fed the 2.36 inch rocket into its back and armed the weapon. "You're good."

Sam looked through the cross hairs of the bazooka's telescope, aimed, and squeezed the firing trigger.

A large plume of orange flame gushed from the back of the rocket, as it hurled towards the Mercedes up ahead.

Missing the vehicle by half a foot, the rocket found its target — a large rock up in front and to the left of the truck.

The missile head penetrated the rock, and then exploded a moment later.

The driver of the Mercedes swerved, but he was too late, and the blast shockwave threw the car on its side, where it rolled several times and then came to a stop on its roof.

Sam's father slammed on the brakes, coming to a stop just beside the destroyed Mercedes.

Tom looked down at the wreckage. "I don't know Sam; I think Aliana's still going to be pretty pissed at you."

Sam grabbed the heavy M60 like it was a toy, and said, "Come on, before they realize what's happened," and jumped off the back of the Utility's cargo tray.

He opened the front door, and had the weapon pointed at the driver's head an instant later. Sam recognized the man as being the engineer named Byron. He looked confused, and there was more than a trickle of blood coming out the man's ears as he looked up. A quick scan of the inside of the vehicle showed that the man was alone.

Sam dragged him out, and away from the burning car, "Where is she? Where does he have Aliana?" The man didn't say a word.

Sam punched him in the gut, careful to avoid accidentally killing him in anger before he got what he wanted. Byron then vomited blood, but said nothing. He was either too injured to speak or was refusing. Either way, the man was useless to him.

Sam didn't have time to deal with him — he needed answers.

"The Merc's empty and there's nothing that suggests where the other one went," Tom said.

"All right, they must have taken multiple cars. Let's keep following the tracks and . . ." Sam stopped talking, as he spotted a Mercedes coming at him at full speed.

He and Tom both pulled out their M9 machine guns and started firing at the driver. The bullets appeared to disappear into the truck's outer shell harmlessly.

Rodriguez had obviously paid top dollar for military grade armor.

Sam recognized the driver as Frank, the dwarf-like miner who'd helped him locate the fake Mahogany Ship. The man looked crazy as he drove towards them, a sense of invincibility radiating as the rapid fire bullets raked his windscreen.

Frank's intention was clear — he was going to run them both down.

Sam looked about, only to realize that they had left it too late, and had nowhere to take cover.

The truck came hurtling towards them.

They dropped their weapons as they began running towards the Holden. Behind them, they heard the crunch as the truck drove straight through Byron, who had been too confused to know what was going to happen to him.

Sam expected his own bones to crunch in a split second.

Then he saw the flash and turned.

The tank piercing M9 rocket had burned its way inside the Mercedes's engine block. A split second later the entire thing erupted in a ball of fire and shrapnel.

Behind him, James, put the bazooka down and said, "Boom — look at that thing explode!"

Sam wasted no time trying to plan his next move. With the remains of both six-wheelers still burning, the three men got back into the Holden and continued to follow the trail.

Picking up his cell, Sam called Elise.

"Hello, Sam." The voice sounded younger than he'd imagined. More like a girl in her early twenties than a woman. He'd never actually spoken to her. In fact, he'd often wondered whether Elise was simply an alias. In the years that he'd used her services, he'd always done so through a secure internet connection at her direction. "You must be in trouble." she said.

She had intentionally kept their relationship untraceable, but given him the number to call, if he ever became desperate.

Now was one of those times.

"You were right. Rodriguez is an asshole, and he's taken Aliana. I need you to find him before he leaves the country."

"Okay. Where was he last seen?" she asked. Sam could hear her feverishly tapping away at her keyboard, most likely accessing a number of overhead satellites.

"He was driving a grey six-wheel Mercedes, somewhere near our current location, about half an hour ago. I'll just read you my GPS coordinates."

"Don't bother, I've already acquired them from your cell phone."

Sam gripped the edge of the car for stability, as his father swung around another corner.

"Oh, Sam, what have you been doing?" Elise said, as if she were admonishing a child. "You've left two burning trucks, and at least one dead person . . . there'll be an investigation, you know."

"We can deal with that later. Right now, I need to know where Rodriguez has gone — can't you track Aliana's cell phone or something?"

"No, it's signal disappeared about twenty miles to the north, presumably where she was captured, perhaps? Hang on, I'm trying something else . . . okay, got it."

"Where?"

"Someone's started warming up the engines on his jet at Bendigo airport . . ."

"But is Aliana there?"

"No, but if its engines are turning over, they must be expecting him. I'll run a search within fifty miles of the airport."

James turned on to the blacktop and headed towards Bendigo. The speedometer, Sam noticed, was creeping upwards, and was reaching for a hundred miles per hour.

"Okay, found him. He's thirty miles out of Bendigo."

Sam pulled out the GPS on his phone. "We're 80 miles away. There's no way we're going to make it in time. Can you stall the plane's takeoff?"

Elise laughed, "I appreciate the vote of confidence, Sam, but there's nothing I can do to convince a privately own A380 that it doesn't want to take off."

"What about the police? Can you send them a false terrorist threat or something?"

"That could be arranged, not that it would do much good. The airport is empty and the nearest police are 80 miles away."

The Holden started to shudder with vibrations as it reached the 100 mile-per-hour mark.

"All right, we'll try our best. Can you find if they've lodged a flight plan, maybe we can cut him off at his destination?"

"Sorry, nothing logged yet."

"Okay, thanks Elise, call me back as soon as you know anything."

"Will do."

Forty-five minutes later, they arrived at the back runway of the Bendigo airport.

At the far end of the airport, the gigantic, specialized, A380 looked unnatural in its surroundings. In fact, had it been the standard, commercial model, the plane would have had nowhere near enough runway to take off, but Rodriguez had obviously had it built specifically to decrease its takeoff distance.

"There!" Sam pointed it out before they'd even driven into the grounds of the airport.

James turned the car and drove straight through the wired fence designed to keep wildlife off the runway, "I see them."

Giant dust spirals, fifty feet high, were forming, behind the airbus.

"They're getting ready to take off!" James said.

And then it started moving towards them.

Sam reached for his machine gun, and pointed it towards the front of the plane.

The plane began picking up speed.

His finger began squeezing the trigger.

Tom pulled it downward, and a number of bullets sprayed the ground ahead. "It's started the takeoff. Anything you do now will just get her killed!"

James, pulled the car off to the side of the runway, as the nose of the plane left the runway.

Sam swore and punched the dashboard. "We lost her!"

He felt Tom's hand on his shoulder. "It's all right, we'll find out where they're headed, and then someone will be waiting for them when they land."

Two hours later, Sam received a call from Elise.

"Have you got their destination?" he asked, immediately.

"No, and there's something else you're not going to like."

"What?"

"I tracked Rodriguez's plane as it made a direct route eastward until it was a hundred and fifty miles off the coast . . ." she then stopped.

"Then what?"

"And then it disappeared."

"What do you mean it disappeared?"

"I mean, I could hack into the Australian radar towers and track its progress over land, and tracked her transponder, and maintained a visual of her movement via satellite. But once it was out of radar range, it headed towards dense cloud cover. The pilot switched off its transponder, and changed directions. I'm trying to pick its signal up again, but it appears to have disappeared completely."

"You lost it? The world's largest commercial jet, and you can find it with all of the data at your fingertips?" Sam said.

"It's a big ocean. I'll keep trying, but whoever's flying this thing's a professional."

"Okay, keep trying. You can't move an A380 without someone noticing it."

James looked at him, and for the first time in Sam's life, his father looked uncertain about their next move.

"It's your show, son. Where do you want to go?"

"Oh my god!" Sam said, "I just worked out where he's headed."

Both Tom and James simultaneously said, "Where?"

Sam ignored their question and got Elise back on the line. "I need you to find me the closest and fastest jet."

"Military or private?"

"I don't care, whatever's closest. Rodriguez already has a two-hour head start."

A moment later, Elise said, "There's a Citation X — it's not a lot faster than the A380, but it's been fitted with long range fuel tanks so at least you won't have to land and refuel."

"That's great — where?"

"One's currently sitting in a private hangar at Elmore airport, about twenty-minute drive from where you are."

"That'll do. Find the owner for me and tell them I'm taking their jet," Sam then sent Elise a text with the details of his flight, using Tom's smartphone. "I've sent you the details where I want to go, and what I'm bringing into the country — I need you to clear everything with the required government officials."

There was a momentary pause, as Elise skimmed the text. "I'll do my best Sam, but their government's not going to be happy with you bringing machine guns."

"I know. Just pay their bribes, and make it happen."

CHAPTER 22

Billie looked at the wall along the base of the sarcophagus for what must have been the thousandth time since discovering the looking glass. She could identify a little over half the pictographs, and all but three of the locations seen through it.

Somewhere, on this wall, were the answers to all her questions. The questions her grandfather had instilled in her when she was just six years old. Deep inside the inner psyche of her mind, Billie knew that she was close.

Then she saw it.

Standing above the sarcophagus, she noticed that the pictographs weren't just maps to direct the lens of the looking glass — they were actual maps to each of the locations.

From where they were in the middle, the images above were in the northern hemisphere, whereas those below, were situated in the southern.

She still couldn't understand how they knew about them, and even recorded some that weren't yet built at the time of this pyramid's creation.

Making a couple calculations, she tried to pinpoint the distance between two places that she knew, starting with the submerged pyramid, where she stood, and the pyramid of Giza. Once she'd worked it out, she found the ratio between actual distance and the map.

Then, she measured the distance between where she stood, and pictograph of Stonehenge, and applied the same ratio. Afterwards, she calculated the known distance between Stonehenge and where she was standing.

They were an exact match, give or take a single mile.

Fuck me – that means I can work out exactly where Atlantis lies!

Billie began to measure, so that she could work out the primitive distance.

And then the alarm went off.

"Billie, come in!"

She jumped down and picked up the radio.

"What is it, Veyron?"

"Two torpedoes, coming in fast, approximately 30 miles away."

Shit, they found me quicker than I thought!

They were getting smarter, or was she getting slower?

"Copy that..."

"You may still have time to get out!"

"I doubt that," Billie said and she reached into her duffle bag, retrieving a laser cutter.

It was going to break her heart, but she had to cut the top of the round lens off the looking glass. It was the only lead that she might ever have—that's if she even survived the next couple minutes.

She attached the mechanical frame to the looking glass and switched on the laser. It might take a few minutes to slice through.

While it was heating up, Billie jumped back down and grabbed her laptop.

There was no time, for anything . . .

All her work was there.

Everything would have amounted to nothing if she didn't get it.

She removed the hard drive and slid it into her watertight pocket. Then she climbed back up the sarcophagus, held the laser cutter, and removed the lens to the looking glass. It could have been a beautiful blue diamond, but to her, it was much more valuable.

A sound like thunder striking a hundred times at once, echoed throughout the pyramid.

For a second, she thought that it was going to take the beating as the entire structure shuddered like an earthquake — and then something cracked.

Water began trickling in from the roof.

Slow at first, and then faster, and then water poured in with the pressure of a high powered jet, before rocks started to fall.

She had to get out now if she was going to have any chance of survival, but she was trapped. Leaning with her back against the wall, she watched in horror as the roof above her split in two. Water, along with giant rocks, now decimated the King's Chamber.

Billie reached for her dive mask, and jumped through the tunnel below. With nothing to stop the pressure of the water below from rising, now that the roof of the pyramid had collapsed, water now filled the chambers below — rising with the force of nearly 500 feet of water above.

Her hand reached for the rope ladder, stopping her before

she hit the second chamber, swinging her into the middle.

More blocks and water came down, flooding the entire pyramid with debris.

Until nothing remained.

Aliana looked at the man pointing the gun at her. Where she'd seen an intelligent, confident, and powerful man a week ago, she now saw a child who'd never had any real friends, who was forever trying to supersede his father's success.

And she saw a man turned delirious with desire.

Men, in the midst of insanity, she knew, were the most dangerous of all. He pointed towards the base of the pyramid. "Start climbing," he said.

"You want me to climb the Great Pyramid of Giza?"

He pointed the gun towards her and then fired a single shot. It struck the wall behind her, shattering the face of the limestone. "I won't ask you again."

She turned and looked at the pyramid above, and tried to remember the height of the only remaining wonder of the Seven Wonders of the Ancient World.

It was irrelevant—with her climbing experience, the trip would probably kill Rodriguez first.

Aliana then started to climb.

Followed by several local men who Rodriguez had bribed to give him access and carry the Ark of Light.

By eleven a.m. the sun was gaining on the horizon, and the temperature was rising. Not quite as hot as yesterday's top of

118 degrees Fahrenheit, it was already well above 100. Sam swallowed a mouthful of water, pausing between limestone blocks, and then continued to climb.

"Are you certain he's aiming for the top?" Tom asked.

"Pretty sure."

"Because, maybe we could just wait down the bottom for him?"

Sam ignored the question, and took some more climbing chalk out of his bag to dry his hands. Then, studying the difficult handhold above, he reached up and then swung his legs onto the next limestone block.

"I don't know what you're complaining about, Tom. You can practically step up this damn pyramid."

More than fifty blocks above them, Sam spotted the reflection of light.

Was it them, or had I imagined it?

The light reflecting off the Ark of Light then glistened like a star. "Come on Tom. It's them, and they've got a big lead on us."

Aliana watched Rodriguez hold the Ark of Light up. It was approaching midday, and soon the sun would be directly overhead.

"Put it down, Rodriguez. It's over," she heard Sam's voice, from below.

"Sam!" she shouted, in relief.

Rodriguez fired several shots from his massive handgun, blowing apart large chunks of the pyramid's block.

"I have to give it to you, Sam, you seem like a difficult man to kill. But, you must know, you're too late—it's nearly midday, and I'm about to receive all the knowledge and power of man. There's nothing more you can do." He stood up and raised the Ark of Light so that its powerful diamond faced the sun, rapidly approaching overhead.

"No, you can't!" Sam yelled.

Aliana took a step back, and then jumped off the top level of the pyramid to the blocks several feet below.

"Get back here, woman," Rodriguez shouted. "Don't you understand once I receive this power, there's nothing you or Reilly can do to stop me?"

With her arms still bound, she jumped down the next one.

"Aliana!" She heard Sam's voice in the distance. "Duck!"

"Good bye mortals," Rodriguez said, as the sun came into a direct line above him.

She crouched down, taking cover as close to the block of the pyramid as she could, shielding herself with her arms over her head.

The world above opened into the most magnificent light she'd ever seen, and for an instant, she thought that it had all been real. That Rodriguez had won; that in this instant, he was gaining all the power and knowledge of the human race, throughout time.

Then a sound like thunder struck the top of the pyramid.

The stunning light turned to such extreme heat that the entire capstone of the pyramid exploded.

And then it all passed.

The sun continued on its way, and above, there was only quiet.

Sam climbed up the last block below her and took her in his

arms. "You're alive."

"Of course I am. I told you to wait for me when I dived for it, but this time you're the one who disappeared."

She kissed him, and it felt good.

Resting her head on his chest, with his arms around her, she was home, with the man she loved.

Aliana then whispered, "What happened to him?"

"He's dead."

"Why? I thought that the Ark of Light was supposed to bring its owner omnipotent powers?"

"Yes, but only those worthy, who could read the ancient texts, and understand when exactly to use it."

"And for those who aren't worthy?" she asked.

"Those are the fallen ones."

CHAPTER 23

At the base of the pyramid, James was waiting for them, a luxury limousine ready to take them back to the airport.

James asked, "So, what did it cost you in the end?"

"What?"

"The map. What did Jie Qiang want for it?"

"He said that he wanted Rodriguez to get everything he'd ever wanted, and then, at that moment, have it all taken away from him."

"I'd say Jie Qiang would be happy for the outcome, wouldn't you?"

Tom had been at home in California for less than a day, and already, he was keen to return to the Maria Helena. Sam and James had both told him to take some time off and enjoy himself. They'd all been through a lot over the past month.

It was only 8 a.m. and the sun was already warm. He could go to the beach, have a surf, and enjoy the day, but he couldn't quite relax. He'd never been very good at it.

Matthew had called from aboard the Maria Helena to tell

him that the cleanup of the hydrogen cyanide was well on its way, and that it might take a few years for the sea life to return to normal in the Gulf of Mexico—but thanks to him and Sam the place would survive.

Tom asked again if they'd had any news of Billie's body, and was advised that it was unlikely they'd ever find her. After all, the entire pyramid imploded under the enormous weight of the ocean, after it lost its structure.

Death had been common enough in his life, but he'd learned to deal with it by burying himself deeper with work, not having a holiday and moping.

It was time to go out, and do something different, he decided.

He grabbed his wallet, glasses, and keys to his Ducati—the motorcycle's equivalent of a Lamborghini—and opened the front door.

And there she stood.

"It's you." Tom didn't know what else to say.

"And you," she replied, stupidly. "Who the hell were you expecting?"

"You're alive!" he said throwing his arms around her.

She stepped forward, a little closer to his face, and said, "Of course. That wasn't the first time they've tried to kill me since Sam and I started this thing."

He stepped backwards, until she'd followed him inside.

Then, closing the door behind her, Billie reached up on the tips of her toes, wrapped her arms around his strong neck, and an inch before reaching his lips, asked, "Did you miss me?"

"Yes," was all he replied, before their lips touched.

Tom kissed her as much as he'd wanted to since their first

night inside the Mayan pyramid.

And soon the kissing turned to undressing.

Tom pulled back for a moment, with his arms still wrapped around her tiny waist, as he admired her in nothing but underwear. They were white and cotton—nothing that suggested they were designed to be sexy—but over her tall, lithe, body and olive skin, they might as well have been intended for a lingerie model. Her body, in complete proportion, had an athletic build, with firm, small breasts.

She looked as amazing in her underwear as he'd imagined a thousand times by now.

Billie stared back at him, a coy and flirtatious smile below the teasing glint in her almond eyes, in response to Tom's blatant adoration of her figure. She slid her underwear off, and said, "Did you just want to look at me, or are you going to fuck me?"

Tom rolled over with a fright.

How long had they been in bed?

It was dark outside. Checking his bedside clock, he saw that it was already after midnight.

"What is it?" she whispered, rolling on her side and exposing her perfect, small, breasts. "Is everything okay?"

"Yes, of course. It's better than okay," he replied, grinning as he stared at her again. "It's just that I don't know how I'm going to break this one to Sam, that's all."

"Why?"

"You know . . ." he hinted.

"No, I don't know?"

"You two. Your history together."

"Did you think Sam and I were lovers?"

"Yes, weren't you?"

"Christ no!"

"But you said you and Sam had an unbelievable past?"

"We do, and if you and I are still alive by the end of the year, I'll tell you the entire story."

Sam boarded his father's Gulfstream at LAX.

He knew what was coming and decided to head to Washington to deal with it before they came to him. Stopped at the end of the runway, the pilot increased the engine's power in preparation for takeoff, and then shut it down completely.

Sam stood up to find out what was wrong, but had a terrible gut feeling he already knew.

"Your guest, Mr. Reilly."

"Then you'd better send her in," Sam said, not waiting to ask who had stopped his jet.

He remained sitting, while the woman walked along the sleek interior of the plane. Her slim, yet overriding figure taking his breath away.

Despite his complete distrust of the woman in front of him, he couldn't help but admit, that for one of the most powerful women on earth, she was by far the sexiest redhead he'd ever met — not that it made their meetings any more pleasant. After all, she'd expressed on many occasions how that sentiment was mutual.

His mind quickly considered the events of the past month, and he wondered what, precisely, she was going to go after.

Behind her strong jawbone, starry blue eyes, dark, short-cropped hair, and genuinely attractive face, Sam thought her perfect smile somehow always appeared halfway between beautiful and a constant scowl. At times, he wondered whether that, too, was a mask that came with the position.

"Good morning, Madam Secretary," he said, standing up.

"Sit down, Mr. Reilly," she commanded. "Tell me, what did you find in the Gulf of Mexico?"

So, that's what this is about?

He was glad his father had hidden the Ark of Light before anyone acknowledged it had even been discovered.

"Very little. As you know, Madam Secretary, you destroyed all of it."

"We did?" She shook her head. "No, Mr. Reilly, I assure you, if we wanted its secrets destroyed, that stupid girlfriend of yours, Dr. Swan, wouldn't have survived."

"Not you?" Sam was genuinely surprised. "Then who?"

"Someone else who's been closing in on our hunt for the Master Builders. And you'd better pray, you beat them to it."

"If they were as powerful as I'm starting to believe, we'd better all pray that our enemies don't discover them first." Sam laughed. "So Billie's still alive?"

The Secretary of Defense ignored his question, as she so often did.

"Oh, and Dr. Swan's not my girlfriend."

The U.S. Secretary of Defense smiled. Her perfect white teeth, glaring, and replied, "Yes, Mr. Reilly, we know all about your history with that girl. Do you think that by sending her there while you went in search of the Mahogany Ship, it would keep us from finding out the truth?"

He shuffled his feet uncomfortable in the seat, and then replied, "I had hoped so."

"So, do you have another lead?"

"Not yet, but I'm hoping, if Billie is alive, she will make contact soon," he said. "Perhaps when I return from Washington?"

"You're not going to Washington. There's no one there who wants to speak with you. I suggest you turn your father's toy airplane around, and go home."

"As you wish, Madam Secretary."

At 2 a.m. Billie turned up at his house. Despite the U.S. Secretary of Defense suggesting she was still alive, he hadn't completely believed it.

"Jesus, Billie," he said, throwing his arms around her. "I was starting to think you were actually dead!"

"Yeah, well, that's what they would have liked, wouldn't they?" she replied, quickly removing his arms from her torso. She studied his face, and then said, "Damn it, you knew they would come, didn't you?"

He turned to avoid her gaze.

"When Rodriguez asked me to help him find the Mahogany Ship I had personal reasons to go searching for it. Specifically, it was the first shipwreck that my father and I ever hunted together. My feelings were tied because I really did want to know more about the sunken Mayan pyramid."

"But you knew that the Master Builders were involved!"

"No. Well, not at first. I reluctantly agreed to think about going with Rodriguez on his expedition. It was only when I replayed the recording I'd made of the king's sarcophagus that

I saw the image of the Mahogany Ship on the wall."

"And then you realized that the Mahogany Ship was built by the Master Builders!"

"That's right. And I knew I had to distance myself from the discovery as fast as possible. I hoped they would assume that if I'd discovered anything of value, then surely I wouldn't have left the project to someone else. Giving you enough time to find some answers. Instead, now all we have are more questions."

"I might just have one answer . . ."

"What about?"

"The communication device . . . it was made out of a stone, not too dissimilar to a diamond in chemical makeup."

"How could you have possibly done that? Everything was destroyed?"

"Yes, but before that happened, I broke off a little."

He examined the stone, which fit comfortably in the palm of his hand. It looked like an enormous blue diamond. Even with today's technologies, nothing even resembling its brilliance could be synthetically manufactured.

It sparkled in his hand under the limited light of the night lamp.

"Is it a diamond?"

"No. I've taken it to three leading experts in geology. None of them can tell me what is, only what it isn't."

"And what's that?"

"It's not synthetically made, and it's never been seen before."

Sam looked at it again, wondering in the back of his mind if he'd somehow seen a similar stone, somewhere else. "Could they tell you anything about the type of stone it resembles, other than a very sparkling diamond?"

"They each identified that it has some unusual properties."

"Such as?"

"The stone transmits light and sound more than a thousand times faster than water. And is the first naturally occurring substance harder than diamond."

"Interesting. I suppose that explains how it was used to see other parts of the Mayan pyramid," he said.

Billie laughed, "You and I both know that's not true, don't we?"

Ignoring her statement, he said, "So we lost the greatest lead for Master Builders we've ever had?"

"Yes."

"And it was all for nothing, with exception of the discovery of the best fake diamond the world has ever seen?"

"No." Billie smiled, holding her hard drive. "Because I think I just found a map to Atlantis."

The End

Want more?

Join my email list and get a FREE and EXCLUSIVE Sam Reilly story that's not available anywhere else!

Join here ~ http://bit.ly/ChristopherCartwright

Printed in Great Britain
by Amazon